THE ADVENTURES OF ULYSSES

Illustrated

CHARLES LAMB

ntents

THE ADVENTURES OF ULYSSES

With Illustrations by
N. H. Squire & E. Mars

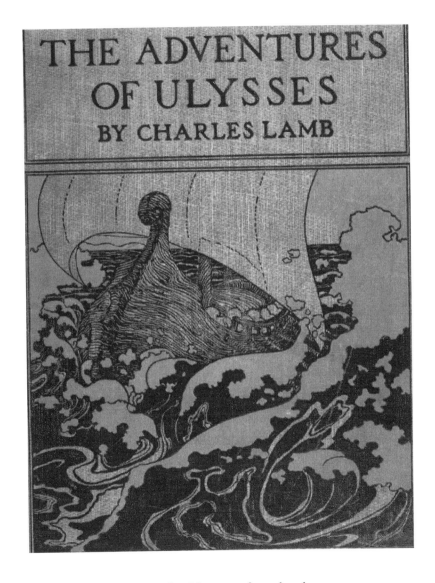

Edited, with notes for schools

New York
R. H. RUSSELL
1902

Preface

NONE, except those who have carefully considered the subject, can rightly estimate the difficulty of selecting suitable English prose books for the younger children in our schools. There are many books written in recent years well suited for class work; but they are practically prohibited, owing to copyright, the high price of publication, and the form in which they are necessarily issued. Most of the children's books, of an earlier date, can hardly be said to belong to literature. *The Adventures of Ulysses,* though not so well known as it ought to be, has held its position, and I have long desired to see it introduced into school use. It gave me, therefore, no little pleasure, when the present publishers placed it in my hands to be issued as one of their Intermediate School Series. Of its suitability as such, there can be no doubt. It deals with what has well been called "the current coin of the world's intercourse;" it is written by one of the greatest masters of English prose; and it was published specially for children. It appeals fully to the fancy and imagination, faculties which in youth are too often neglected, but which, when rightly cultivated, are the most fertile fields for true and lasting educational results.

I have taken an editor's liberty with the punctuation, for the purpose of giving more ease to the text, which Lamb's too frequent use of the colon rendered in many places heavy and involved. In no case have I made a change where the sense could be considered to suffer. I have made also a very few slight alterations which the demands of a school text rendered necessary. The quotations from Chapman will clearly show how close Lamb kept to his translation of the *Odyssey,* thus giving a quaint charm and old-world air to his prose.

The few will, doubtless, consider I have erred in giving too great fulness to the Notes; but it is done from the judgment bought by experience of what the many will require.

John Cook, 1892

Introduction

THE writer of this book was Charles Lamb. He was born in 1775, in one of the quaint courts of the group of buildings belonging to the lawyers in London, known as the Temple. When a child of seven he was sent to Christ's Hospital, where the boys have to dress in long dark-blue coats, yellow stockings, and shoes, and go hatless, after the fashion of the time of Edward VI., who founded that school. When Lamb grew up he became a clerk, but he soon took to writing books. His sister was able to assist him, and with her he wrote several for children, as, *Tales from Shakespere,* and *Poetry for Children.* By himself he wrote, in the year 1808, this book, *The Adventures of Ulysses,* whose story is one of the oldest and best tales in the world. Lamb was very fond of our old English literature, and he wrote very clever essays on the plays written at the time of Queen Elizabeth. He wrote also many essays about himself, and the London world in which he lived and moved. They are so beautifully and truthfully told, that we know more about him than almost any other writer; and he is, in consequence, one of the most loved of all those who have made us wiser, happier, and better by their books.

Homer, who is generally considered the writer of the book from which the *Adventures of Ulysses* is taken, is called the "Prince of Poets," because he is the greatest epic poet--that is, writer about heroes, wars, and adventures--that ever lived. He lived in Greece, but so long ago that no one can tell exactly when, but probably about one thousand years before Christ was born. The place of birth too is not known, but he was so celebrated that many cities contended for the honour of having him as their citizen. Some say he was blind; but he could not always have been so. A blind man could never have sung of the sea and its foaming waves; of the beautiful scenery of rocky shores and sea-girt islands; of the sky, the fields, and the woods, unless he at one time had good powers of sight. His occupation was that of a wandering minstrel which was then considered a very honourable calling, and continued to be for very many centuries afterwards all over Europe. The greatest respect was shown to these minstrels. Kings and princes and other important persons gave them welcome, and listened as they sang of the deeds of great men, whether describing those of their ancestors, their relatives, or their own; and they showed their pleasure by giving presents of money or costly gifts. We owe a great deal of our knowledge of history and men to these singers. They put into verse the great deeds of heroes in wars, sieges, battles, and adventures, and they were handed down by word of mouth until someone put them into writing. Homer's poems were composed at a time in which there was, perhaps, no writing, or very little; but the singers had good memories, and were practised in the art of learning by rote.

We may safely assume that much of the great stories told by Homer existed before his time, but not in the beautiful form in which we have it from him. Just as a painter takes the colours scattered on his palette, and works them into a picture on his canvas, or a woman the many-coloured threads of silk from her basket, and produces a beautiful piece of needlework, so Homer took the mixed tales of gods, heroes, travel, battle, and war, and by the exercise of his great powers of language, fancy, and imagination, weaved them into the greatest poem ever written. His work is all the more wonderful since he had no model to follow; and although he had afterwards many imitators none have ever surpassed, or perhaps even equalled him. His knowledge of human nature was so great, that the best men in all ages have been glad to learn wisdom from him. In Greece boys learned his poems at school; many men could boast of knowing his poems by heart, and wherever a Greek went, he carried a love and reverence of the great poet with him. The ancients long after he was dead had such reverence for him, that they held festivals in his honour, raised temples and altars to him, offered sacrifices, and worshipped him as a god. The great charm in Homer lies in the artless and simple way in which he relates his story, and describes the varying incidents in the lives of his heroes. But his poems are chiefly valuable to us for the important lessons we learn of the manners, customs, and mode of life of the ancient Greeks, and the social conditions under which they lived. When he described all these, and sang of battles, sieges, deeds of arms, and of sacrifices to the gods, the people understood him because it related to their every-day life, and not to a time long gone by.

Homer's two great poems are the *Iliad*, so called because it treats of the great siege of Ilios or Troy; and the *Odyssey*, because it tells of the wanderings, or adventures of Odysseus or Ulysses, the name by which he is best known. These two poems are divided into twenty-four books, being the same number as the letters of the Greek alphabet. The world as known to the ancient Greeks formed but a very small portion of the world as known to us. They knew the rocky shores, promontories, and islands of their own country, the coast of Asia Minor, the shores of Egypt, and the south of Italy, round which Homer leads Ulysses in his wanderings. They peopled strange lands with giants, monsters, and cannibals, and located the gods whom they worshipped in distant mountains, islands, woods, and caves. Their notion of the world was that it was flat; and that far beyond all known countries it was bounded by a great sea river called Oceanus, across which the souls of the dead passed and for ever dwelt in gloomy and misty regions, shrouded from the sweet light of heaven. The living could not cross this ocean and return; but by the interference of a goddess Ulysses was given this privilege, as Homer describes.

The gods of the Greeks were many, and they governed the destinies of men. Ruler of all was Jupiter, who is often described as sitting in his court with all the gods in council, on Olympus, a mountain of Macedonia and Thessaly, whose top the ancients thought touched the heavens and where reigned an eternal spring. Jupiter had power over the elements, and hurled his thunderbolts and lightning against offending men. Juno was his wife, the queen of heaven, and Minerva, the goddess of wisdom, his daughter, who befriended Ulysses and his son Telemachus. Neptune ruled the sea, and could shake kingdoms with his earthquakes. Pluto ruled over hell, and all that lay under the earth, and with his brothers, Jupiter and Neptune, shared the kingdom of their father Saturn. Æolus had power over the winds, and befriended Ulysses. Diana was the goddess of the chase, and is generally represented in a hunting habit attended with dogs. Venus was the goddess of love and beauty; Mars was the god of war; Apollo, the god of poetry; and very many others. There were also various classes of female deities, called nymphs, presided over mountains, hills, dales, the sea, rivers, fountains, streams, and lakes; living often in woods, caverns, or grottos, amid most enchanting scenes. The gods were gifted with like passions as men, and interfered in the most wonderful way in all human affairs. Homer tells of the constant interest manifested by many of them in the siege of Troy, and how they frequently took part in the battles, some siding with the Trojans, and some with the Greeks. Indeed it was not possible for one who had offended any of the deities to escape terrible punishment, unless protected by one mightier than they.

An examination of a map of Greece will show what a great extent of coast-line it has, no other country in Europe exceeding it in this respect. It is surrounded on all sides by the sea, except the north. Its shores are much indented, many bays and gulfs extending deeply inland, and far-reaching rocky promontories projecting into the sea. Most of the Greek states had easy communication by means of the sea. The inhabitants were great mariners, as Ulysses was, and fond of adventure. The country is highly mountainous, lofty ranges separating many plains where the principal cities were situated, and which became the centres of separate and independent states. The rocky shores of the sea-girt land, the rugged and broken outline of its mountain chains, and the beautiful atmosphere which clothes external nature, have made the scenery of Greece celebrated in all ages. Under such conditions would be developed a free and independent spirit in its people, attended with poetical and intellectual gifts; so that the Greeks became in time most highly civilized, and gave to the world the richest treasures of learning, science, and art.

Greece, at this early period, was not a united country ruled by one king. It contained as many monarchs, or princes, as there were towns, who united to fight common foes, but very often they engaged in petty warfare among themselves. Many of the cities in time became celebrated for the cultivation of art, science, learning, and civilization, such as Athens, Corinth, Sparta, Thebes, Delphi, and others. The ancient Greeks were remarkable for their bravery in time of war; they gloried to show their valour in the fight, and were indifferent to wounds, or death received in the field of battle. Their armour consisted of shields, helmets, spears, and swords, beautifully ornamented in gold and silver, and they wore greaves also upon their legs. A sword given to Ulysses, at the court of King Alcinous, had a handle of massive silver, and its sheath was of ivory. Much value was set upon the arms of a hero, as his life largely depended on them, and when he died they were often given to another, as we read of Ulysses getting those of Achilles, and for ever making an enemy of Ajax thereby.

In those times the king had absolute power; he was the leader in battle, the judge in all disputes, the priest who offered sacrifices and prayers to the gods for the people. It was necessary for him to be brave and heroic in order to maintain his position and authority; otherwise he could not command the respect of his subjects, or prevent the invasion and plunder of his city or state by jealous or ambitious neighbours. He had to be an orator, too, and to cultivate the art of making eloquent speeches upon great occasions, such as the beginning of a battle; and the soldiers despised the leader who could not rouse up their passions to fight, in a stirring and spirited oration, or lead them with mighty voice to the onset.

The king had his council of chiefs, to whom he imparted his intentions, and consulted with on all important matters; but he was not obliged to follow their advice unless he liked. He was not above personal labour. Ulysses could build a ship, and navigate it with sails and oars; he made and fitted up his own bed; he could plough the land, and work in the fields. But war was more indulged in by kings and people than the arts of peace. They fought with great cruelty, and plundered and burned towns and cities without mercy. When a great foe was killed, his arms became the spoils of the victor. The Greek chiefs pierced the dead body of Hector, while Achilles tied it, by the feet, to his chariot, dragged it, in view of his father, mother, wife, and friends, three times each morning round the tomb of Patroclus, and kept it twelve days unburied. Human sacrifices were not unknown, and Achilles offered up twelve Trojan captive youths at the funeral rites of Patroclus, his friend and companion in arms.

The habits of the people were simple and temperate, and all ate of the same kind of food. Their meat was the flesh of oxen, sheep, goats, and swine; kings' sons were often shepherds, and their chief riches consisted in the flocks which they reared. Corn was grown, from which bread was made, and served out to the guests in baskets. Fruits were also used at meals, and they drank wine mixed with water. Before drinking, a portion was poured out as an offering to the gods. They were very hospitable to strangers, as we find Ulysses most kindly received by King Alcinous and Eumæus the herdsman, and entertained with the best food and drink they could place before him; for, as the latter says, "Poor men are all from Jove commended to our entertaining love." At their banquets the minstrel played on the harp, and sang; on festive occasions they danced skilful measures; and the youths engaged in friendly contests, in running, wrestling, throwing quoits, and shooting with the bow.

The members of the family were bound together by the closest ties. The authority of the father over all was complete, and the children dreaded giving him offence, or bringing upon them his anger or his curse. Though wives were bought in exchange for oxen, sheep, or other valuable things, they exercised much liberty, and were highly thought of; as will be gathered from the story of Ulysses' return to Penelope, after an absence of twenty years. They were skilful in spinning and needlework, as well as in all other domestic affairs; and even kings' daughters, with their maidens, washed the household clothes in the river, as we read of Nausicaa, the daughter of Alcinous, doing when she met Ulysses.

The people at this time lived mostly in towns, strongly fortified, surrounded with walls, amid gardens, palaces, and temples. The houses of the kings and chiefs were built of stone, and finely ornamented, furnished with beautiful vessels of gold, silver, bronze, and earthenware, and the walls hung with armour. Without was a great court in which games were played, having in the centre an altar for sacrifices. Carving in stone was done at this time; but the beautiful statues of gods and goddesses that we see in galleries and pictures, and which we read of in books, belong to a much later time than that of Homer. Though his description of buildings, and the style in which kings and chiefs lived, may at times be exaggerated, such as that of the palace of king Alcinous and his court, it is yet certain that great advances had been made in civilization at the time; and many beautiful things have been discovered amid the ruins of ancient Greece, showing the people to have expended much skill and industry in their production.

Now to understand how it came about that Ulysses had to set forth on his wanderings, it is necessary to relate briefly the events that preceded it. There was a king of Thessaly, named Peleus, who married a sea goddess named Thetis. All the deities were invited to the marriage festival except the goddess of Discord; and to show her envy at the slight, she threw an apple among them with the words "to be given to the fairest" written on it. There was a keen contention then over to whom it was to be given; but Juno, Venus, and Minerva were the chief claiments. The gods unwilling to become judges in so delicate a matter, appointed Paris, a son of Priam, King of Troy, in Asia Minor, then a shepherd on mount Ida, near that city, to decide who was the fairest of the three. Juno promised him a kingdom, Minerva great military renown, and Venus the fairest woman in the world for a wife, if he decided in their favour. He at last gave his decision in favour of Venus, which drew upon him and the Trojans the anger of the disappointed goddesses.

The most beautiful woman in the world, at the time, was Helen, the daughter of Leda, wife of Tyndarus, King of Lacedæmon in the south-east coast of Greece. So celebrated was she, that the most noted of the Greek princes sought her in marriage, a compliment which alarmed rather than pleased Tyndarus. Among them was Ulysses, prince of Ithaca, a small and rocky island in the Ionian sea, east of the larger island of Cephalonia. He was known then for his wisdom, prudence, and eloquence; and, fearing that he would not be successful, he offered to advise Tyndarus how to get out of his difficulty, if he would grant him his niece Penelope in marriage. To this Tyndarus agreed, and Ulysses then advised him that he should bind all the princes to a solemn promise, that they would consent to Helen's own free choice, and to defend and protect her in future against any danger. The princes all agreed and made promise; and Helen selected Menelaus, King of Sparta, and married him. Shortly afterwards Paris visited Lacedæmon, on pretence of offering sacrifices to Apollo. He was most kindly received by Menelaus, and while the latter was on an expedition to Crete, Paris enticed Helen to fly with him to Troy; and thus he got possession of her whom Venus had promised as a reward for the decision in her favour. Menelaus, on his return, was enraged at the loss of his wife, and appealed to the Greek princes for help, and reminded them of their promise. They readily consented to avenge the outrage that had been committed, as they looked upon it as if it had been done to themselves. They first sent messengers to Priam, demanding back Helen, which the king refused. They then commenced preparations for war, fitted out a fleet of 1,200 ships, carrying 100,000 men, and sailed across the Ægean sea to Troy. Agamemnon, King of Argos and Mycenae, and brother to Menelaus, was selected leader of the expedition; but the kings and princes acted as counsellors on all important occasions. Among the celebrated Greek chiefs were Achil The siege of Troy lasted ten years, but the *Iliad* of Homer only deals with the events of the last year. A quarrel occurred between Achilles and Agamemnon; and Achilles retired from the siege, and a great pestilence seized upon the Greek camp. The Trojans beat back the Greeks, and then Achilles was prevailed upon to give his armour to his friend Patroclus, who charged the enemy at the head of the Myrmidons. Patroclus was killed in the contest, at which Achilles was filled with great grief and rage. He offered his services anew to revenge the death of his friend and companion, and he killed Hector in single combat, with whose burial the *Iliad* closes. Achilles was killed by an arrow shot by Paris, but directed by Apollo. It wounded him in the heel, the only place in which he was vulnerable. Paris, too, the cause of all the woe, was killed, and Troy soon fell by a strategem of Ulysses. By his device a wooden horse was built, inside which lay concealed a number of armed men. The Trojans brought the horse into the city; and at night the Greeks came out and opened the ates for their companions, who now put the inhabitants to the sword, and burned the city. Menelaus returned with Helen to his own city, but Agamemnon returned only to be murdered as Homer tells. Ulysses, alone of those who survived, had not returned to his rocky home, where his aged father, Laertes, Penelope, his wife, and his son Telemachus, whom he had left an infant, so long awaited him. Driven by storms from shore to shore, he and his companions encountered many misfortunes, and incurred the great anger of Neptune, for the injury inflicted on his son, Polyphemus the Cyclop. After suffering many distresses and losing all his companions, he remained for seven years in the enchanted abode of the goddess Calypso. Befriended by Minerva, he was at last released, and after enduring much further hardship, he found himself at last on the shores of Ithaca, after an absence of twenty years. All this Homer describes in the *Odyssey*, which has been put into prose in this book. The poem closes with the triumph of Ulysses over all his enemies, and his happy union with his wife and father, after so long and cruel a separation.

John Cook, 1892

Introduction by Charles Lamb

THIS work is designed as a supplement to the *Adventures of Telemachus*. It treats of the conduct and sufferings of Ulysses, the father of Telemachus. The picture which it exhibits is that of a brave man struggling with adversity; by a wise use of events, and with an inimitable presence of mind under difficulties, forcing out a way for himself through the severest trials to which human life can be exposed; with enemies natural and preternatural surrounding him on all sides. The agents in this tale, besides men and women, are giants, enchanters, sirens: things which denote external force or internal temptations, the twofold danger which a wise fortitude must expect to encounter in its course through this world. The fictions contained in it will be found to comprehend some of the most admired inventions of Grecian mythology.

The ground-work of the story is as old as the *Odyssey*, but the moral and the colouring are comparatively modern. By avoiding the prolixity which marks the speeches and the descriptions in *Homer*, I have gained a rapidity to the narration, which I hope will make it more attractive, and give it more the air of a romance to young readers; though I am sensible that by the curtailment I have sacrificed in many places the manners to the passion, the subordinate characteristics to the essential interest of the story. The attempt is not to be considered as seeking a comparison with any of the direct translations of the *Odyssey*, either in prose or verse, though if I were to state the obligations which I have had to one obsolete version, *[note]* I should have run the hazard of depriving myself of the very slender degree of reputation which I could hope to acquire from a trifle like the present undertaking.

* The translation of Homer, in verse, by George Chapman, a celebrated poet in the time of Elizabeth and James I. Lamb says of him, "He would have made a great epic poet, if, indeed, he has not abundantly shown himself to be one, for his Homer is not so properly a translation as the stories of Achilles and Ulysses rewritten. The earnestness and passion which he has put into every part of these poems would be incredible to a reader of more modern translations."

Charles Lamb

Chapter 1

The Cicons. The fruit of the Lotos-tree. Polyphemus and the Cyclops. The Kingdom of the Winds, and God Æolus's fatal present. The Læstrygonian Man-eaters.

THIS history tells of the wanderings of Ulysses and his followers in their return from Troy after the destruction of that famous city of Asia by the Grecians. He was inflamed with a desire of seeing again, after a ten years' absence, his wife and native country Ithaca. He was king of a barren spot, and a poor country, in comparison of the fruitful plains of Asia which he was leaving, or the wealthy kingdoms which he touched upon in his return; yet wherever he came, he could never see a soil which appeared in his eyes half so sweet or desirable as his country earth. This made him refuse the offers of the goddess Calypso to stay with her, and partake of her immortality, in the delightful island; and this gave him strength to break from the enchantments of Circe, the daughter of the Sun.

From Troy ill winds cast Ulysses and his fleet upon the coast of the Cicons, a people hostile to the Grecians. Landing his forces, he laid siege to their chief city, Ismarus, which he took, and with it much spoil, and slew many people. But success proved fatal to him; for his soldiers, elated with the spoil, and the good store of provisions which they found in that place, fell to eating and drinking, forgetful of their safety, till the Cicons, who inhabited the coast, had time to assemble their friends and allies from the interior; who mustering in prodigious force, set upon the Grecians, while they negligently revelled and feasted, and slew many of them, and recovered the spoil. They, dispirited and thinned in their numbers, with difficulty made their retreat good to the ships.

Thence they set sail, sad at heart, yet something cheered that with such fearful odds against them they had not all been utterly destroyed. A dreadful tempest ensued, which for two nights and two days tossed them about, but the third day the weather cleared, and they had hopes of a favourable gale to carry them to Ithaca; but as they doubled the Cape of Malea, suddenly a north wind arising, drove them back as far as Cythera. After that, for the space of nine days, contrary winds continued to drive them in an opposite direction to the point to which they were bound, and the tenth day they put in at a shore where a race of men dwell that are sustained by the fruit of the lotos-tree. Here Ulysses sent some of his men to land for fresh water, who were met by certain of the inhabitants, that gave them some of their country food to eat; not with any ill intention towards them, though in the event it proved pernicious; for, having eaten of this fruit, so pleasant it proved to their appetite, that they in a minute quite forgot all thoughts of home, or of their countrymen, or of ever returning back to the ships to give an account of what sort of inhabitants dwelt there, but they would needs stay and live there among them, and eat of that precious food for ever; and when Ulysses sent others of his men to look for them, and to bring them back by force, they strove, and wept, and would not leave their food for heaven itself, so much the pleasure of that enchanting fruit had bewitched them. But Ulysses caused them to be bound hand and foot, and cast under the hatches; and set sail with all possible speed from that baneful coast, lest others after them might taste the lotos, which had such strange qualities to make men forget their native country, and the thoughts of home.

Coasting on all that night by unknown and out of the way shores, they came by day-break to the land where the Cyclops dwell, a sort of giant shepherds that neither sow nor plough, but the earth untilled produces for them rich wheat and barley and grapes, yet they have neither bread nor wine, nor know the arts of cultivation, nor care to know them: for they live each man to himself, without laws or government, or anything like a state or kingdom; but their dwellings are in caves, on the steep heads of mountains, every man's household governed by his own caprice, or not governed at all, their wives and children as lawless as themselves, none caring for others, but each doing as he or she thinks good. Ships or boats they have none, nor artificers to make them, no trade or commerce, or wish to visit other shores; yet they have convenient places for harbours and for shipping. Here Ulysses with a chosen party of twelve followers landed, to explore what sort of men dwelt there, whether hospitable and friendly to strangers, or altogether wild and savage, for as yet no dwellers appeared in sight.

The first sign of habitation which they came to was a giant's cave rudely fashioned, but of a size which betokened the vast proportions of its owner, the pillars which supported it being the bodies of huge oaks or pines, in the natural state of the tree, and all about showed more marks of strength than skill in whoever built it. Ulysses, entering in, admired the savage contrivances and artless structure of the place, and longed to see the tenant of so outlandish a mansion; but well conjecturing that gifts would have more avail in extracting courtesy, than strength could succeed in forcing it, from such a one as he expected to find the inhabitant, he resolved to flatter his hospitality with a present of Greek wine, of which he had store in twelve great vessels; so strong that no one ever drank it without an infusion of twenty parts of water to one of wine, yet the fragrance of it even then so delicious, that it would have vexed a man who smelled it to abstain from tasting it; but whoever tasted it, it was able to raise his courage to the height of heroic deeds. Taking with them a goat-skin flagon full of this precious liquor, they ventured into the recesses of the cave. Here they pleased themselves a whole day with beholding the giant's kitchen, where the flesh of sheep and goats lay strewed, his dairy where goat-milk stood ranged in troughs and pails, his pens where he kept his live animals; but those he had driven forth to pasture with him when he went out in the morning. While they were feasting their eyes with a sight of these curiosities, their ears were suddenly deafened with a noise like the falling of a house. It was the owner of the cave who had been abroad all day feeding his flock, as his custom was, in the mountains, and now drove them home in the evening from pasture. He threw down a pile of firewood, which he had been gathering against suppertime, before the mouth of the cave, which occasioned the crash they heard. The Grecians hid themselves in the remote parts of the cave, at sight of the uncouth monster. It was Polyphemus, the largest and savagest of the Cyclops, who boasted himself to be the son of Neptune. He looked more like a mountain crag than a man, and to his brutal body he had a brutish mind answerable. He drove his flock, all that gave milk, to the interior of the cave, but left the rams and the he-goats without. Then taking up a stone so massy that twenty oxen could not have drawn it, he placed it at the mouth of the cave, to defend the entrance, and sat him down to milk his ewes and his goats; which done, he lastly kindled a fire, and throwing his great eye round the cave (for the Cyclops have no more than one eye, and that placed in the midst of their forehead), by the glimmering light he discerned some of Ulysses' men.

"Ho, guests, what are you? merchants or wandering thieves?" he bellowed out in a voice which took from them all power of reply, it was so astounding.

Only Ulysses summoned resolution to answer, that they came neither for plunder nor traffic, but were Grecians who had lost their way, returning from Troy; which famous city, under the conduct of Agamemnon, the renowned son of Atreus, they had sacked, and laid level with the ground. Yet now they prostrated themselves humbly before his feet, whom they acknowledged to be mightier than they, and besought him that he would bestow the rites of hospitality upon them, for that Jove was the avenger of wrongs done to strangers, and would fiercely resent any injury which they might suffer.

"Fool," said the Cyclop, "to come so far to preach to me the fear of the gods. We Cyclops care not for your Jove, whom you fable to be nursed by a goat, nor any of your blessed ones. We are stronger than they, and dare bid open battle to Jove himself, though you and all your fellows of the earth join with him." And he bade them tell him where their ship was, in which they came, and whether they had any companions. But Ulysses, with a wise caution, made answer, that they had no ship or companions, but were unfortunate men whom the sea, splitting their ship in pieces, had dashed upon his coast, and they alone had escaped. He replied nothing, but griping two of the nearest of them, as if they had been no more than children, he dashed their brains out against the earth, and (shocking to relate) tore in pieces their limbs, and devoured them, yet warm and trembling, making a lion's meal of them, lapping the blood: for the Cyclops are *man-eaters*, and esteem human flesh to be a delicacy far above goat's or kid's; though by reason of their abhorred customs few men approach their coast except some stragglers, or now and then a shipwrecked mariner. At a sight so horrid, Ulysses and his men were like distracted people. He, when he had made an end of his wicked supper, drained a draught of goat's milk down his prodigious throat, and lay down and slept among his goats. Then Ulysses drew his sword, and half resolved to thrust it with all his might in at the bosom of the sleeping monster; but wiser thoughts restrained him, else they had there without help all perished, for none but Polyphemus himself could have removed that mass of stone which he had placed to guard the entrance. So they were constrained to abide all that night in fear.

When day came the Cyclop awoke, and kindling a fire, made his breakfast of two other of his unfortunate prisoners, then milked his goats as he was accustomed, and pushing aside the vast stone, and shutting it again when he had done, upon the prisoners, with as much ease as a man opens and shuts a quiver's lid, he let out his flock, and drove them before him with whistlings (as sharp as winds in storms) to the mountains.

Then Ulysses, of whose strength or cunning the Cyclop seems to have had as little heed as of an infant's, being left alone, with the remnant of his men which the Cyclop had not devoured, gave manifest proof how far manly wisdom excels brutish force. He chose a stake from among the wood which the Cyclop had piled up for firing, in length and thickness like a mast, which he sharpened and hardened in the fire, and selected four men, and instructed them what they should do with this stake, and made them perfect in their parts.

When the evening was come, the Cyclop drove home his sheep; and as fortune directed it, either of purpose, or that his memory was overruled by the gods to his hurt (as in the issue it proved), he drove the males of his flock, contrary to his custom, along with the dams into the pens. Then shutting-to the stone of the cave, he fell to his horrible supper. When he had dispatched two more of the Grecians Ulysses waxed bold with the contemplation of his project, and took a bowl of Greek wine, and merrily dared the Cyclop to drink.

"Cyclop," he said, "take a bowl of wine from the hand of your guest; it may serve to digest the man's flesh that you have eaten, and show what drink our ship held before it went down. All I ask in recompense, if you find it good, is to be dismissed in a whole skin. Truly you must look to have few visitors, if you observe this new custom of eating your guests."

The brute took and drank, and vehemently enjoyed the taste of wine, which was new to him, and swilled again at the flagon, and entreated for more, and prayed Ulysses to tell him his name, that he might bestow a gift upon the man who had given him such brave liquor. The Cyclops (he said) had grapes, but this rich juice (he swore) was simply divine. Again Ulysses plied him with the wine, and the fool drank it as fast as he poured out, and again he asked the name of his benefactor, which Ulysses cunningly dissembling, said, "My name is Noman: my kindred and friends in my own country call me Noman." "Then," said the Cyclop, "this is the kindness I will shew thee, Noman: I will eat thee last of all thy friends." He had scarce expressed his savage kindness, when the fumes of the strong wine overcame him, and he reeled down upon the floor, and sank into a dead sleep.

Ulysses watched his time, while the monster lay insensible, and heartening up his men, they placed the sharp end of the stake in the fire till it was heated red-hot, and some god gave them a courage beyond that which they were used to have, and the four men with difficulty bored the sharp end of the huge stake, which they had heated red-hot, right into the eye of the drunken cannibal, and Ulysses helped to thrust it in with all his might, still farther and farther, with effort, as men bore with an auger, till the scalded blood gushed out, and the eye-ball smoked, and the strings of the eye cracked, as the burning rafter broke in it, and the eye hissed, as hot iron hisses when it is plunged into water.

He waking, roared with the pain so loud that all the cavern broke into claps like thunder. They fled, and dispersed into corners. He plucked the burning stake from his eye, and hurled the wood madly about the cave. Then he cried out with a mighty voice for his brethren, the Cyclops, that dwelt hard by in caverns upon hills; they, hearing the terrible shout, came flocking from all parts to inquire what ailed Polyphemus? and what cause he had for making such horrid clamours in the night-time to break their sleep? if his fright proceeded from any mortal? if strength or craft had given him his death's blow? He made answer from within that Noman had hurt him, Noman had killed him, Noman was with him in the cave. They replied, "If no man has hurt thee, and no man is with thee, then thou art alone, and the evil that afflicts thee is from the hand of heaven, which none can resist or help." So they left him and went their way, thinking that some disease troubled him. He, blind and ready to split with the anguish of the pain, went groaning up and down in the dark, to find the doorway, which when he found, he removed the stone, and sat in the threshold, feeling if he could lay hold on any man going out with the sheep, which (the day now breaking) were beginning to issue forth to their accustomed pastures. But Ulysses, whose first artifice in giving himself that ambiguous name, had succeeded so well with the Cyclop, was not of a wit so gross to be caught by that palpable device. But casting about in his mind all the ways which he could contrive for escape (no less than all their lives depending on the success) at last he thought of this expedient. He made knots of the osier twigs upon which the Cyclop commonly slept, with which he tied the fattest and fleeciest of the rams together, three in a rank, and under the belly of the middle ram he tied a man, and himself last, wrapping himself fast with both his hands in the rich wool of one, the fairest of the flock.

And now the sheep began to issue forth very fast; the males went first, the females unmilked stood by, bleating and requiring the hand of their shepherd in vain to milk them, but he much sorer with the loss of sight. Still as the males passed, he felt the backs of those fleecy fools, never dreaming that they carried his enemies under their bellies; so they passed on till the last ram came loaded with his wool and Ulysses together. He stopped that ram and felt him, and had his hand once in the hair of Ulysses, yet knew it not, and he chid the ram for being last, and spoke to it as if it understood him, and asked it whether it did not wish that its master had his eye again, which that abominable Noman with his execrable rout had put out, when they had got him down with wine; and he willed the ram to tell him whereabouts in the cave his enemy lurked, that he might dash his brains and strew them about, to ease his heart of that tormenting revenge which rankled in it. After a deal of such foolish talk to the beast he let it go.

When Ulysses found himself free, he let go his hold, and assisted in disengaging his friends. The rams which had befriended them they carried off with them to the ships, where their companions with tears in their eyes received them, as men escaped from death. They plied their oars, and set their sails, and when they were got as far off from shore as a voice would reach, Ulysses cried out to the Cyclop, "Cyclop, thou should'st not have so much abused thy monstrous strength, as to devour thy guests. Jove by my hand sends thee requital to pay thy savage inhumanity." The Cyclop heard, and came forth enraged, and in his anger he plucked a fragment of a rock, and threw it with blind fury at the ships. It narrowly escaped lighting upon the bark in which Ulysses sat, but with the fall it raised so fierce an ebb, as bore back the ship till it almost touched the shore. "Cyclop," said Ulysses, "if any ask thee who imposed on thee that unsightly blemish in thine eye, say it was Ulysses, son of Laertes: the king of Ithaca am I called, the waster of cities." Then they crowded sail, and beat the old sea, and forth they went with a forward gale; sad for forepast losses, yet glad to have escaped at any rate; till they came to the isle where Æolus reigned, who is god of the winds.

Here Ulysses and his men were courteously received by the monarch, who showed him his twelve children which have rule over the twelve winds. A month they stayed and feasted with him, and at the end of the month he dismissed them with many presents, and gave to

Ulysses at parting an ox's hide, in which were inclosed *the winds;* he left abroad the western wind, to play upon their sails, and waft them gently home to Ithaca. This bag bound in a glittering silver band, so close that no breath could escape, Ulysses hung up at the mast. His companions did not know its contents, but guessed that the monarch had given to him some treasures of gold or silver.

Nine days they sailed smoothly, favoured by the western wind, and by the tenth they approached so nigh as to discern lights kindled on the shores of their country earth; when, by ill-fortune, Ulysses, overcome with fatigue of watching the helm, fell asleep. The mariners seized the opportunity, and one of them said to the rest, "A fine time has this leader of ours; wherever he goes he is sure of presents, when we come away empty-handed; and see, what king Æolus has given him, store no doubt of gold and silver." A word was enough to those covetous wretches, who quick as thought untied the bag, and instead of gold, out rushed with mighty noise *the winds.* Ulysses with the noise awoke and saw their mistake, but too late, for the ship was driving with all the winds back far from Ithaca, far as to the island of Æolus from which they had parted, in one hour measuring back what in nine days they had scarcely tracked, and in sight of home too! Up he flew amazed, and raving doubted whether he should not fling himself into the sea for grief of his bitter disappointment. At last he hid himself under the hatches for shame. And scarce could he be prevailed upon, when he was told he was arrived again in the harbour of king Æolus, to go himself, or send to that monarch for a second succour; so much the disgrace of having misused his royal bounty (though it was the crime of his followers and not his own) weighed upon him. And when at last he went, and took a herald with him, and came where the god sat on his throne, feasting with his children, he would not trust in among them at their meat, but set himself down like one unworthy in the threshold.

Indignation seized Æolus to behold him in that manner returned; and he said, "Ulysses, what has brought you back? are you so soon tired of your country? or did not our present please you? we thought we had given you a kingly passport." Ulysses made answer; "My men have done this ill mischief to me: they did it while I slept." "Wretch," said Æolus, "avaunt, and quit our shores: it fits not us to convoy men whom the gods hate, and will have perish."

Forth they sailed, but with far different hopes than when they left the same harbour the first time with all the winds confined, only the west-wind suffered to play upon their sails to waft them in gentle murmurs to Ithaca. They were now the sport of every gale that blew, and despaired of ever seeing home more. Now those covetous mariners were cured of their surfeit for gold, and would not have touched it if it had lain in untold heaps before them.

Six days and nights they drove along, and on the seventh day they put into Lamos, a port of the Læstrygonians. So spacious this harbour was, that it held with ease all their fleet, which rode at anchor, safe from any storms, all but the ship in which Ulysses was embarked. He, as if prophetic of the mischance which followed, kept still without the harbour, making fast his bark to a rock at the land's point, which he climbed with purpose to survey the country. He saw a city with smoke ascending from the roofs, but neither ploughs going, nor oxen yoked, nor any sign of agricultural works. Making choice of two men, he sent them to the city to explore what sort of inhabitants dwelt there. His messengers had not gone far before they met a damsel, of stature surpassing human, who was coming to draw water from a spring. They asked her who dwelt in that land. She made no reply, but led them in silence to her father's palace. He was a monarch and named Antiphas. He and all his people were giants. When they entered the palace, a woman, the mother of the damsel, but far taller than she, rushed abroad and called for Antiphas. He came, and snatching up one of the two men, made as if he would devour him. The other fled. Antiphas raised a mighty shout, and instantly, this way and that, multitudes of gigantic people issued out at the gates, and making for the harbour, tore up huge pieces of the rocks, and flung them at the ships which lay there, all which they utterly overwhelmed and sank; and the unfortunate bodies of men which floated, and which the sea did not devour, these cannibals thrust through with harpoons, like fishes, and bore them off to their dire feast. Ulysses with his single bark that had never entered the harbour escaped; that bark which was now the only vessel left of all the gallant navy that had set sail with him from Troy. He pushed off from the shore, cheering the sad remnant of his men, whom horror at the sight of their countrymen's fate had almost turned to marble.

Chapter 2

The house of Circe. Men changed into beasts. The voyage to Hell. The banquet of the Dead.

ON went the single ship till it came to the island of Ææa, where Circe the dreadful daughter of the Sun dwelt. She was deeply skilled in magic, a haughty beauty, and had hair like the Sun.

Here a dispute arose among Ulysses' men, which of them should go ashore and explore the country; for there was a necessity that some should go to procure water and provisions, their stock of both being nigh spent; but their hearts failed them when they called to mind the shocking fate of their fellows whom the Læstrygonians had eaten, and those whom the foul Cyclop Polyphemus had crushed between his jaws; which moved them so tenderly in the recollection that they wept. But tears never yet supplied any man's wants, this Ulysses knew full well, and dividing his men (all that were left) into two companies, at the head of one of which was himself, and at the head of the other Eurylochus, a man of tried courage, he cast lots which of them should go up into the country, and the lot fell upon Eurylochus and his company, two and twenty in number; who took their leave, with tears, of Ulysses and his men that stayed, whose eyes wore the same wet badges of weak humanity, for they surely thought never to see these their companions again, but that on every coast where they should come, they should find nothing but savages and cannibals.

Eurylochus and his party proceeded up the country, till in a dale they descried the house of Circe, built of bright stone, by the road's side. Before her gate lay many beasts, as wolves, lions, leopards, which, by her art, of wild, she had rendered tame. These arose when they saw strangers, and ramped upon their hinder paws, and fawned upon Eurylochus and his men, who dreaded the effects of such monstrous kindness; and staying at the gate they heard the enchantress within, sitting at her loom, singing such strains as suspended all mortal faculties, while she wove a web, subtle and glorious, and of texture inimitable on earth, as all the housewiferies of the deities are. Strains so ravishingly sweet, provoked even the sagest and prudentest heads among the party to knock and call at the gate. The shining gate the enchantress opened, and bade them come in and feast. They unwise followed, all but Eurylochus, who stayed without the gate, suspicious that some train was laid for them. Being entered, she placed them in chairs of state, and set before them meal and honey, and Smyrna wine; but mixed with baneful drugs of powerful enchantment. When they had eaten of these, and drunk of her cup, she touched them with her charming-rod, and straight they were transformed into swine, having the bodies of swine, the bristles, and snout, and grunting noise of that animal; only they still retained the minds of men, which made them the more to lament their brutish transformation. Having changed them, she shut them up in her sty with many more whom her wicked sorceries had formerly changed, and gave them swine's food, mast, and acorns, and chestnuts, to eat.

Eurylochus, who beheld nothing of these sad changes from where he was stationed without the gate, only instead of his companions that entered (who he thought had all vanished by witchcraft) beheld a herd of swine, hurried back to the ship, to give an account of what he had seen; but so frightened and perplexed, that he could give no distinct report of anything, only he remembered a palace, and a woman singing at her work, and gates guarded by lions. But his companions, he said, were all vanished.

Then Ulysses, suspecting some foul witchcraft, snatched his sword, and his bow, and commanded Eurylochus instantly to lead him to the place. But Eurylochus fell down, and embracing his knees, besought him by the name of a man whom the gods had in their protection, not to expose his safety, and the safety of them all, to certain destruction.

"Do thou then stay, Eurylochus!" answered Ulysses: "eat thou and drink in the ship in safety; while I go alone upon this adventure: necessity, from whose law is no appeal, compels me."

So saying he quitted the ship and went on shore, accompanied by none; none had the hardihood to offer to partake that perilous adventure with him, so much they dreaded the enchantments of the witch. Singly he pursued his journey till he came to the shining gates which stood before her mansion; but when he essayed to put his foot over her threshold, he was suddenly stopped by the apparition of a young man, bearing a golden rod in his hand, who was the god Mercury. He held Ulysses by the wrist, to stay his entrance; and "Whither wouldst thou go?" he said; "O, thou most erring of the sons of men! knowest thou not that this is the house of great Circe, where she keeps thy friends in a loathsome sty, changed from the fair forms of men into the detestable and ugly shapes of swine? art thou prepared to share their fate, from which nothing can ransom thee?" But neither his words, nor his coming from heaven, could stop the daring foot of Ulysses, whom compassion for the misfortune of his friends had rendered careless of danger; which when the god perceived, he had pity to see valour so misplaced, and gave him the flower of the herb *moly*, which is sovereign against enchantments. The moly is a small unsightly root, its virtues but little known, and in low estimation; the dull shepherd treads on it every day with his clouted shoes; but it bears a small white flower, which is medicinal against charms, blights, mildews, and damps. "Take this in thy hand," said Mercury, "and with it boldly enter her gates; when she shall strike thee with her rod, thinking to change thee, as she has changed thy friends, boldly rush in upon her with thy sword, and extort from her the dreadful oath of the gods, that she will use no enchantments against thee; then force her to restore thy abused companions." He gave Ulysses the little white flower, and instructing him how to use it, vanished.

When the god was departed, Ulysses with loud knockings beat at the gate of the palace. The shining gates were opened, as before, and great Circe with hospitable cheer invited in her guest. She placed him on a throne with more distinction than she had used to his fellows, she mingled wine in a costly bowl, and he drank of it, mixed with those poisonous drugs. When he had drunk, she struck him with her charming-rod, and "To your sty," she cried; "out, swine; mingle with your companions." But those powerful words were not proof against the preservative which Mercury had given to Ulysses; he remained unchanged, and as the god had directed him, boldly charged the witch with his sword, as if he meant to take her life: which when she saw, and perceived that her charms were weak against the antidote which Ulysses bore about him, she cried out and bent her knees beneath his sword, embracing his, and said, "Who or what manner of man art thou? Never drank any man before thee of this cup, but he repented it in some brute's form. Thy shape remains unaltered as thy mind. Thou canst be none other than Ulysses, renowned above all the world for wisdom, whom the Fates have long since decreed that I must love."

"O Circe," he replied, "how canst thou treat of love or marriage with one whose friends thou hast turned into beasts? and now offerest him thy hand in wedlock, only that thou mightest have him in thy power, subject to thy will, perhaps to be advanced in time to the honour of a place in thy sty. What pleasure canst thou promise, which may tempt the soul of a reasonable man? thy meats, spiced with poison; or thy wines drugged with death? Thou must swear to me, that thou wilt never attempt against me the treasons which thou hast practised upon my friends." The enchantress, won by the terror of his threats, or by the violence of that new love which she felt kindling in her veins for him, swore by Styx, the great oath of the gods, that she meditated no injury to him. Then Ulysses made show of gentler treatment, which gave her hopes of inspiring him with a passion equal to that which she felt. She called her handmaids, four that served her in chief, who were daughters to her silver fountains, to her sacred rivers, and to her consecrated woods, to deck her apartments, to spread rich carpets, and set out her silver tables with dishes of the purest gold, and meat as precious as that which the gods eat, to entertain her guest. One brought water to wash his feet, and one brought wine to chase away, with a refreshing sweetness, the sorrows that had come of late so thick upon him, and hurt his noble mind. They strewed perfumes on his head, and after he had bathed in a bath of the choicest aromatics they brought him rich and costly apparel to put on. Then he was conducted to a throne of massy silver, and a regale, fit for Jove when he banquets, was placed before him. But the feast which Ulysses desired was to see his friends (the partners of his voyage) once more in the shapes of men; and the food which could give him nourishment must be taken in at his eyes. Because he missed this sight, he sat melancholy and thoughtful, and would taste of none of the rich delicacies placed before him. Which when Circe noted, she easily divined the cause of his sadness, and leaving the seat in which she sat throned, went to her sty, and led abroad his men, who came in like swine, and filled the ample hall, where Ulysses sat, with gruntings. Hardly had he time to let his sad eye run over their altered forms and brutal metamorphosis, when with an ointment which she smeared over them, suddenly their bristles fell off, and they started up in their own shapes men as before. They knew their leader again, and clung about him with joy of their late restoration, and some shame for their late change; and wept so loud, blubbering out their joy in broken accents, that the palace was filled with a sound of pleasing mourning, and the witch herself, great Circe, was not unmoved at the sight. To make her atonement complete, she sent for the remnant of Ulysses' men who stayed behind at the ship, giving up their great commander for lost; who when they came, and saw him again alive, circled with their fellows, no expression can tell what joy they felt; they even cried out with rapture, and to have seen their frantic expressions of mirth, a man might have supposed that they were just in sight of their country earth, the cliffs of rocky Ithaca. Only Eurylochus would hardly be persuaded to enter that palace of wonders, for he remembered with a kind of horror how his companions had vanished from his sight.

Then great Circe spake, and gave order, that there should be no more sadness among them, nor remembering of past sufferings. For as yet they fared like men that are exiles from their country, and if a gleam of mirth shot among them, it was suddenly quenched with the thought of their helpless and homeless condition. Her kind persuasions wrought upon Ulysses and the rest, that they spent twelve months in all manner of delight with her in her palace. For Circe was a powerful magician, and could command the moon from her sphere, or unroot the solid oak from its place to make it dance for their diversion, and by the help of her illusions she could vary the taste of pleasures, and contrive delights, recreations, and jolly pastimes, to "fetch the day about from sun to sun, and rock the tedious year as in a delightful dream."

At length Ulysses awoke from the trance of the faculties into which her charms had thrown him, and the thought of home returned with tenfold vigour to goad and sting him; that home where he had left his virtuous wife Penelope, and his young son Telemachus. One day when Circe had been lavish of her caresses, and was in her kindest humour, he moved to her subtly, and as it were afar off, the question of his home-return; to which she answered firmly, "O Ulysses, it is not in my power to detain one whom the gods have destined to further trials. But leaving me, before you pursue your journey home, you must visit the house of Hades, or Death, to consult the shade of Tiresias the Theban prophet; to whom alone, of all the dead, Proserpine, queen of hell, has committed the secret of future events: it is he that must inform you whether you shall ever see again your wife and country." "O Circe," he cried, "that is impossible; who shall steer my course to Pluto's kingdom? Never ship had strength to make that voyage." "Seek no guide," she replied; "but raise you your mast, and hoist your white sails, and sit in your ship in peace: the north wind shall waft you through the seas, till you shall cross the expanse of the ocean, and come to where grow the poplar groves, and willows pale, of Proserpine; where Pyriphlegethon and Cocytus and Acheron mingle their waves. Cocytus is an arm of Styx, the forgetful river. Here dig a pit, and make it a cubit broad and a cubit long, and pour in milk, and honey, and wine, and the blood of a ram, and the blood of a black ewe, and turn away thy face while thou pourest in, and the dead shall come flocking to taste the milk and the blood; but suffer none to approach thy offering till thou hast enquired of Tiresias all which thou wishest to know."

He did as great Circe had appointed. He raised his mast, and hoisted his white sails, and sat in his ship in peace. The north wind wafted him through the seas, till he crossed the ocean, and came to the sacred woods of Proserpine. He stood at the confluence of the three floods, and digged a pit, as she had given directions, and poured in his offering; the blood of a ram, and the blood of a black ewe, milk, and honey, and wine; and the dead came to his banquet: aged men, and women, and youths, and children who died in infancy. But none of them would he suffer to approach, and dip their thin lips in the offering, till Tiresias was served, not though his own mother was among the number, whom now for the first time he knew to be dead, for he had left her living when he went to Troy, and she had died since his departure, and the tidings never reached him: though it irked his soul to use constraint upon her, yet in compliance with the injunction of great Circe, he forced her to retire along with the other ghosts. Then Tiresias, who bore a golden sceptre, came and lapped of the offering, and immediately he knew Ulysses, and began to prophesy: *he denounced woe to Ulysses, woe, woe, and many sufferings, through the anger of Neptune for the putting out of the eye of the sea-god's son. Yet there was safety after suffering, if they could abstain from slaughtering the oxen of the Sun after they landed in the Triangular island. For Ulysses, the gods had destined him from a king to become a beggar, and to perish by his own guests, unless he slew those who knew him not.*

This prophecy, ambiguously delivered, was all that Tiresias was empowered to unfold, or else there was no longer place for him; for now the souls of the other dead came flocking in such numbers, tumultuously demanding the blood, that freezing horror seized the limbs of the living Ulysses, to see so many, and all dead, and he the only one alive in that region. Now his mother came and lapped the blood, without restraint from her son, and now she knew him to be her son, and enquired of him why he had come alive to their comfortless habitations. And she said that affliction for Ulysses' long absence had preyed upon her spirits, and brought her to the grave.

Ulysses' soul melted at her moving narration, and forgetting the state of the dead, and that the airy texture of disembodied spirits do not admit of the embraces of flesh and blood, he threw his arms about her to clasp her: the poor ghost melted from his embrace, and looking mournfully upon him vanished away.

Then saw he Alcmena, the mother of Hercules, and Leda, the wife of Tyndarus, the mother of the beautiful Helen, and of the two brave brothers, Castor and Pollux, who obtained this grace from Jove, that being dead, they should enjoy life alternately, living in pleasant places under the earth. For Pollux had prayed that his brother Castor, who was subject to death, as the son of Tyndarus, should partake of his own immortality, which he derived from an immortal sire: this the Fates denied; therefore Pollux was permitted to divide his immortality with his brother Castor, dying and living alternately. There was Iphimedeia, mother of the giants, Otus and Ephialtes. Earth in her prodigality never nourished bodies to such portentous size and beauty as these two children were of, except Orion. At nine years old they had imaginations of climbing to heaven to see what the gods were doing; they thought to make stairs of mountains, and were for piling Ossa upon Olympus, and setting Pelion upon that, and had perhaps performed it, if they had lived till they were striplings; but they were cut off by death in the infancy of their ambitious project. Phædra was there, and Procris, and Ariadne, mournful for Theseus' desertion, and Eriphyle.

But now came a mournful ghost, that late was Agamemnon, son of Atreus, the mighty leader of all the host of Greece and their confederate kings that warred against Troy. He came with the rest to sip a little of the blood at that uncomfortable banquet. Ulysses was moved with compassion to see him among them, and asked him what untimely fate had brought him there, if storms had overwhelmed him coming from Troy, or if he had perished in some mutiny by his own soldiers at a division of the prey.

"By none of these," he replied, "did I come to my death, but slain at a banquet to which I was invited by Ægisthus after my return home. He conspiring with my wife, they laid a scheme for my destruction, training me forth to a banquet as an ox goes to the slaughter, and there surrounding me they slew me with all my friends about me.

"Clytemnestra, my wicked wife, forgetting the vows which she swore to me in wedlock, would not lend a hand to close my eyes in death. But nothing is so heaped with impieties as such a woman, who would kill her spouse. When I brought her home to my house a bride, I hoped in my heart that she would be loving to me and to my children. Now, her black treacheries have cast a foul aspersion on her whole sex. Blest husbands will have their loving wives in suspicion for her bad deeds."

"Alas!" said Ulysses, "there seems to be a fatality in your royal house of Atreus, and that they are hated of Jove for their wives. For Helen's sake, your brother Menelaus' wife, what multitudes fell in the wars of Troy!"

Agamemnon replied, "For this cause be not thou more kind than wise to any woman. Let not thy words express to her at any time all that is in thy mind, keep still some secrets to thyself. But thou by any bloody contrivances of thy wife never needs't fear to fall. Exceeding wise she is, and to her wisdom she has a goodness as eminent; Icarius' daughter, Penelope the chaste. We left her a young bride when we parted from our wives to go to the wars, with her infant child Telemachus, whom you shall see grown up to manhood on your return, and he shall greet his father with befitting welcomes. My Orestes, my dear son, I shall never see again. His mother has deprived his father of the sight of him, and perhaps will slay him as she slew his sire. But what says fame? is my son yet alive? lives he in Orchomen, or in Pylus? or is he resident in Sparta, in his uncle's court? as yet, I see, divine Orestes is not here with me."

To this Ulysses replied that he had received no certain tidings where Orestes abode, only some uncertain rumours which he could not report the truth.

While they held this sad conference, with kind tears striving to render unkind fortunes more palatable, the soul of great Achilles joined them. "What desperate adventure has brought Ulysses to these regions," said Achilles, "to see the end of dead men and their foolish shades?"

Ulysses answered him that he had come to consult Tiresias respecting his voyage home. "But thou, O son of Thetis," said he, "why dost thou disparage the state of the dead?

eeing that as alive thou didst surpass all men in glory, thou must needs retain thy pre-eminence here below: so great Achilles triumphs over death."

But Achilles made reply that he had much rather be a peasant-slave upon the earth than reign over all the dead. So much did the inactivity and slothful condition of that state displease his unquenchable and restless spirit. Only he inquired of Ulysses if his father Peleus were living, and how his son Neoptolemus conducted himself.

Of Peleus Ulysses could tell him nothing; but of Neoptolemus he thus bore witness: "From Scyros I convoyed your son by sea to the Greeks, where I can speak of him, for I knew him. He was chief in council, and in the field. When any question was proposed, so quick was his conceit in the forward apprehension of any case, that he ever spoke first, and was heard with more attention than the older heads. Only myself and aged Nestor could compare with him in giving advice. In battle I cannot speak his praise, unless I could count all that fell by his sword. I will only mention one instance of his manhood. When we sat hid in the belly of the wooden horse, in the ambush which deceived the Trojans to their destruction, I, who had the management of that stratagem, still shifted my place from side to side to note the behaviour of our men. In some I marked their hearts trembling, through all the pains which they took to appear valiant, and in others tears, that in spite of manly courage would gush forth. And to say truth, it was an adventure of high enterprise, and as perilous a stake as was ever played in war's game. But in him I could not observe the least sign of weakness, no tears nor tremblings, but his hand still on his good sword, and ever urging me to set open the machine and let us out before the time was come for doing it; and when we sallied out he was still first in that fierce destruction and bloody midnight desolation of King Priam's city."

This made the soul of Achilles to tread a swifter pace, with high-raised feet, as he vanished away, for the joy which he took in his son being applauded by Ulysses.

A sad shade stalked by, which Ulysses knew to be the ghost of Ajax, his opponent, when living, in that famous dispute about the right of succeeding to the arms of the deceased Achilles. They being adjudged by the Greeks to Ulysses, as the prize of wisdom above bodily strength, the noble Ajax in despite went mad, and slew himself. The sight of his rival turned to a shade by his dispute, so subdued the passion of emulation in Ulysses, that for his sake he wished that judgment in that controversy had been given against himself, rather than so illustrious a chief should have perished for the desire of those arms, which his prowess (second only to Achilles in fight) so eminently had deserved. "Ajax," he cried, "all the Greeks mourn for thee as much as they lamented for Achilles. Let not thy wrath burn for ever, great son of Telamon. Ulysses seeks peace with thee, and will make any atonement to thee that can appease thy hurt spirit." But the shade stalked on, and would not exchange a word with Ulysses, though he prayed it with many tears and many earnest entreaties. "He might have spoke to me," said Ulysses, "since I spoke to him; but I see the resentments of the dead are eternal."

Then Ulysses saw a throne on which was placed a judge distributing sentence. He that sat on the throne was Minos, and he was dealing out just judgments to the dead. He it is that assigns them their place in bliss or woe.

Then came by a thundering ghost, the large-limbed Orion, the mighty hunter, who was hunting there the ghosts of the beasts which he had slaughtered in desert hills upon the earth; for the dead delight in the occupations which pleased them in their time of living upon the earth.

There was Tityus suffering eternal pains because he offended Latona as she passed from Pytho into Panopeus. Two vultures sat perpetually preying upon his liver with their crooked beaks, which, as fast as they devoured, is for ever renewed; nor can he fray them away with his great hands.

There was Tantalus, plagued for his great sins, standing up to the chin in water, which he can never taste; but still as he bows his head, thinking to quench his burning thirst, instead of water he licks up unsavoury dust. All fruits pleasant to the sight, and of delicious flavour, hang in ripe clusters about his head, seeming as though they offered themselves to be plucked by him; but when he reaches out his hand, some wind carries them far out of his sight into the clouds, so he is starved in the midst of plenty by the righteous doom of Jove, in memory of that inhuman banquet at which the sun turned pale, when the unnatural father served up the limbs of his little son in a dish, as meat for his divine guests.

There was Sisyphus, that sees no end to his labours. His punishment is, to be for ever rolling up a vast stone to the top of a mountain, which when it gets to the top, falls down with a crushing weight, and all his work is to be begun again. He was bathed all over in sweat, that reeked out a smoke which covered his head like a mist. His crime had been the revealing of state secrets.

There Ulysses saw Hercules: not that Hercules who enjoys immortal life in heaven among the gods, and is married to Hebe or Youth, but his shadow which remains below. About him the dead flocked as thick as bats, hovering around, and cuffing at his head: he stands with his dreadful bow, ever in the act to shoot.

There also might Ulysses have seen and spoken with the shades of Theseus, and Pirithous, and the old heroes; but he had conversed enough with horrors, therefore covering his face with his hands, that he might see no more spectres, he resumed his seat in his ship, and pushed off. The barque moved of itself without the help of any oar, and soon brought him out of the regions of death into the cheerful quarters of the living, and to the island of Ææa, whence he had set forth.

Chapter 3

The song of the Sirens. Scylla and Charybdis. The oxen of the Sun. The judgment. The crew killed by lightning.

"UNHAPPY man, who at thy birth wast appointed twice to die! others shall die once: but thou, besides that death that remains for thee, common to all men, hast in thy lifetime visited the shades of death. Thee Scylla, thee Charybdis, expect. Thee the deathful Sirens lie in wait for, that taint the minds of whoever listen to them with their sweet singing. Whosoever shall but hear the call of any Siren, he will so despise both wife and children through their sorceries, that the stream of his affection never again shall set homewards, nor shall he take joy in wife or children thereafter, or they in him."

With these prophetic greetings great Circe met Ulysses on his return. He besought her to instruct him in the nature of the Sirens, and by what method their baneful allurements were to be resisted.

"They are sisters three," she replied, "that sit in a mead (by which your ship must needs pass) circled with dead men's bones. These are the bones of men whom they have slain, after with fawning invitements they have enticed them into their fen. Yet such is the celestial harmony of their voice accompanying the persuasive magic of their words, that knowing this, you shall not be able to withstand their enticements. Therefore when you are to sail by them, you shall stop the ears of your companions with wax, that they may hear no note of that dangerous music; but for yourself, that you may hear, and yet live, give them strict command to bind you hand and foot to the mast, and in no case to set you free, till you are out of the danger of the temptation, though you should entreat it, and implore it ever so much, but to bind you rather the more for your requesting to be loosed. So shall you escape that snare."

Ulysses then prayed her that she would inform him what Scylla and Charybdis were, which she had taught him by name to fear. She replied, "Sailing from Ææa to Trinacria, you must pass at an equal distance between two fatal rocks. Incline never so little either to the one side or the other, and your ship must meet with certain destruction. No vessel ever yet tried that pass without being lost, but the Argo, which owed her safety to the sacred freight she bore, the fleece of the golden-backed ram, which could not perish. The biggest of these rocks which you shall come to, Scylla hath in charge. There, in a deep whirlpool at the foot of the rock, the abhorred monster shrouds her face; who if she were to show her full form, no eye of man or god could endure the sight; thence she stretches out all her six long necks peering and diving to suck up fish, dolphins, dog-fish, and whales, whole ships, and their men, whatever comes within her raging gulf. The other rock is lesser, and of less ominous aspect; but there dreadful Charybdis sits, supping the black deeps. Thrice a day she drinks her pits dry, and thrice a day again she belches them all up; but when she is drinking, come not nigh, for being once caught, the force of Neptune cannot redeem you from her swallow. Better trust to Scylla, for she will but have for her six necks, six men: Charybdis in her insatiate draught will ask all."

Then Ulysses inquired, in case he should escape Charybdis, whether he might not assail that other monster with his sword: to which she replied that he must not think that he had an enemy subject to death, or wounds, to contend with; for Scylla could never die. Therefore, his best safety was in flight, and to invoke none of the gods but Cratis, who is Scylla's mother, and might perhaps forbid her daughter to devour them. For his conduct after he arrived at Trinacria she referred him to the admonitions which had been given him by Tiresias.

Ulysses having communicated her instructions, as far as related to the Sirens, to his companions, who had not been present at that interview; but concealed from them the rest, as he had done the terrible predictions of Tiresias, that they might not be deterred by fear from pursuing their voyage. The time for departure being come they set their sails, and took a final leave of great Circe; who by her art calmed the heavens, and gave them smooth seas, and a right fore wind (the seaman's friend) to bear them on their way to Ithaca.

They had not sailed past a hundred leagues before the breeze which Circe had lent them suddenly stopped. It was stricken dead. All the sea lay in prostrate slumber. Not a gasp of air could be felt. The ship stood still. Ulysses guessed that the island of the Sirens was not far off, and that they had charmed the air so with their devilish singing. Therefore he made him cakes of wax, as Circe had instructed him, and stopped the ears of his men with them: then causing himself to be bound hand and foot, he commanded the rowers to ply their oars, and row as fast as speed could carry them past that fatal shore. They soon came within sight of the Sirens, who sang in Ulysses' hearing:

"Come here, thou, worthy of a world of praise,
That dost so high the Grecian glory raise;
Ulysses! stay thy ship; and that song hear
That none pass'd ever, but it bent his ear,
But left him ravish'd, and instructed more
By us, than any ever heard before.
For we know all things, whatsoever were
In wide Troy labour'd: whatsoever there
The Grecians and the Trojans both sustain'd:
By those high issues that the gods ordain'd:
And whatsoever all the earth can show
To inform a knowledge of desert, we know."

These were the words, but the celestial harmony of the voices which sang them no tongue can describe: it took the ear of Ulysses with ravishment. He would have broke his bonds to rush after them; and threatened, wept, sued, entreated, commanded, crying out with tears and passionate imprecations, conjuring his men by all the ties of perils past which they had endured in common, by fellowship and love, and the authority which he retained among them, to let him loose; but at no rate would they obey him. And still the Sirens sang. Ulysses made signs, motions, gestures, promising mountains of gold if they would set him free; but their oars only moved faster. And still the Sirens sang. And still the more he adjured them to set him free, the faster with cords and ropes they bound him; till they were quite out of hearing of the Sirens' notes, whose effect great Circe had so truly predicted. And well she might speak of them, for often she had joined her own enchanting voice to theirs, while she sat in the flowery meads, mingled with the Sirens and the Water Nymphs, gathering their potent herbs and drugs of magic quality: their singing all together has made the gods stoop, and "heaven drowsy with the harmony."

Escaped that peril, they had not sailed yet an hundred leagues further, when they heard a roar afar off, which Ulysses knew to be the barking of Scylla's dogs, which surround her waist, and bark incessantly. Coming nearer they beheld a smoke ascend, with a horrid murmur, which arose from that other whirlpool, to which they made nigher approaches than to Scylla. Through the furious eddy, which is in that place, the ship stood still as a stone, for there was no man to lend his hand to an oar, the dismal roar of Scylla's dogs at a distance, and the nearer clamours of Charybdis, where everything made an echo, quite taking from them the power of exertion. Ulysses went up and down encouraging his men, one by one, giving them good words, telling them that they were in greater perils when they were blocked up in the Cyclop's cave, yet, heaven assisting his counsels, he had delivered them out of that extremity. That he could not believe but they remembered it; and wished them to give the same trust to the same care which he had now for their welfare. That they must exert all the strength and wit which they had, and try if Jove would not grant them an escape even out of this peril. In particular he cheered up the pilot who sat at the helm, and told him that he must show more firmness than other men, as he had more trust committed to him, and had the sole management by his skill of the vessel in which all their safeties were embarked. That a rock lay hid within those boiling whirlpools which he saw, on the outside of which he must steer, if he would avoid his own destruction, and the destruction of them all.

They heard him, and like men took to the oars; but little knew what opposite danger, in shunning that rock, they must be thrown upon. For Ulysses had concealed from them the wounds, never to be healed, which Scylla was to open; their terror would else have robbed them all of all care to steer, or move an oar, and have made them hide under the hatches, for fear of seeing her, where he and they must have died an idle death. But even then he forgot the precautions which Circe had given him to prevent harm to his person; who had willed him not to arm, or show himself once to Scylla: but disdaining not to venture life for his brave companions, he could not contain, but armed in all points and taking a lance in either hand, he went up to the fore deck, and looked when Scylla would appear.

She did not show herself as yet, and still the vessel steered closer by her rock, as it sought to shun that other more dreaded; for they saw how horribly Charybdis' black throat drew into her all the whirling deep, which she disgorged again, that all about her boiled like a kettle, and the rock roared with troubled waters; which when she supped in again, all the bottom turned up, and disclosed far under shore the swart sands naked, whose all stern sight frayed the startled blood from their faces, and made Ulysses turn his to view the wonder of whirlpools. Which when Scylla saw, from out her black den, she darted out her six long necks, and swoopt up as many of his friends; whose cries Ulysses heard, and saw them too late, with their heels turned up, and their hands thrown to him for succour, who had been their help in all extremities, but could not deliver them now; and he heard them shriek out, as she tore them, and to the last they continued to throw their hands out to him for sweet life. In all his sufferings he never had beheld a sight so full of miseries.

Escaped from Scylla and Charybdis, but with a diminished crew, Ulysses, and the sad remains of his followers reached the Trinacrian shore. Here landing, he beheld oxen grazing of such surpassing size and beauty, that both from them, and from the shape of the island (having three promontories jutting into the sea) he judged rightly that he was come to the Triangular island, and the oxen of the Sun, of which Tiresias had forewarned him.

So great was his terror lest through his own fault, or that of his men, any violence or profanation should be offered to the holy oxen, that even then, tired as they were with the perils and fatigues of the day past, and unable to stir an oar, or use any exertion, and though night was fast coming on, he would have them re-embark immediately, and make the best of their way from that dangerous station. But his men with one voice resolutely opposed it, and even the too cautious Eurylochus himself withstood the proposal; so much did the temptation of a little ease and refreshment (ease tenfold sweet after such labours) prevail over the sagest counsels, and the apprehension of certain evil outweigh the prospect of contingent danger. They expostulated, saying that the nerves of Ulysses seemed to be made of steel, and his limbs not liable to lassitude like other men's; that waking or sleeping seemed indifferent to him; but that they were men, not gods, and felt the common appetites for food and sleep. That in the nighttime all the winds most destructive to ships are generated. That black night still required to be served with meat, and sleep, and quiet havens, and ease. That the best sacrifice to the sea was in the morning. With such sailor-like sayings and mutinous arguments, which the majority have always ready to justify disobedience to their betters, they forced Ulysses to comply with their requisition, and against his will to take up his night-quarters on shore. But he first exacted from them an oath that they would neither maim nor kill any of the cattle which they saw grazing, but content themselves with such food as Circe had stowed their vessel with when they parted from Æaea. This they man by man severally promised, imprecating the heaviest curses on whoever should break it; and mooring their bark within a creek, they went to supper, contenting themselves that night with such food as Circe had given them, not without many sad thoughts of their friends whom Scylla had devoured, the grief of which kept them great part of the night waking.

In the morning Ulysses urged them again to a religious observance of the oath that they had sworn, not in any case to attempt the blood of those fair herds which they saw grazing, but to content themselves with the ship's food; for the god who owned those cattle sees and hears all.

They faithfully obeyed, and remained in that good mind for a month, during which they were confined to that station by contrary winds, till all the wine and the bread were gone, which they had brought with them. When their victuals were gone, necessity compelled them to stray in quest of whatever fish or fowl they could snare, which that coast did not yield in any great abundance. Then Ulysses prayed to all the gods that dwelt in bountiful heaven, that they would be pleased to yield them some means to stay their hunger without having recourse to profane and forbidden violations: but the ears of heaven seemed to be shut, or some god incensed plotted his ruin; for at mid-day, when he should chiefly have been vigilant and watchful to prevent mischief, a deep sleep fell upon the eyes of Ulysses, during which he lay totally insensible of all that passed in the world, and what his friends or what his enemies might do, for his welfare or destruction. Then Eurylochus took his advantage. He was the man of most authority with them after Ulysses. He represented to them all the misery of their condition; how that every death is hateful and grievous to mortality, but that of all deaths famine is attended with the most painful, loathsome, and humiliating circumstances; that the subsistence which they could hope to draw from fowling or fishing was too precarious to be depended upon; that there did not seem to be any chance of the winds changing to favour their escape, but that they must inevitably stay there and perish, if they let an irrational superstition deter them from the means which nature offered to their hands; that Ulysses might be deceived in his belief that these oxen had any sacred qualities above other oxen; and even admitting that they were the property of the god of the Sun, as he said they were, the Sun did neither eat nor drink, and the gods were best served not by a scrupulous conscience, but by a thankful heart, which took freely what they as freely offered. With these and such-like persuasions he prevailed on his half-famished and half-mutinous companions, to begin the impious violation of their oath by the slaughter of seven of the fairest of these oxen which were grazing. Part they roasted and ate, and part they offered in sacrifice to the gods, particularly to Apollo, god of the Sun, vowing to build a temple to his godhead, when they should arrive in Ithaca, and deck it with magnificent and numerous gifts. Vain men! and superstition worse than that which they so lately derided! to imagine that prospective penitence can excuse a present violation of duty, and that the pure natures of the heavenly powers will admit of compromise for sin.

But to their feast they fell, dividing the roasted portions of the flesh, savoury and pleasant meat to them, but a sad sight to the eyes, and a savour of death in the nostrils, of the waking Ulysses; who just woke in time to witness, but not soon enough to prevent, their rash and sacrilegious banquet. He had scarce time to ask what great mischief was this

34

which they had done unto him; when behold, a prodigy! the ox-hides which they had tripped, began to creep, as if they had life; and the roasted flesh bellowed as the ox used to lo when he was living. The hair of Ulysses stood up on end with affright at these omens; but his companions, like men whom the gods had infatuated to their destruction, persisted n their horrible banquet.

The Sun from his burning chariot saw how Ulysses' men had slain his oxen, and he cried to his father Jove, "Revenge me upon these impious men who have slain my oxen, which it did me good to look upon when I walked my heavenly round. In all my daily course I never saw such bright and beautiful creatures as those my oxen were." The father promised that ample retribution should be taken of those accursed men; which was fulfilled shortly after, when they took their leaves of the fatal island.

Six days they feasted in spite of the signs of heaven, and on the seventh, the wind changing, they set their sails, and left the island; and their hearts were cheerful with the banquets they had held; all but the heart of Ulysses, which sank within him, as with wet eyes he beheld his friends, and gave them for lost, as men devoted to divine vengeance. Which soon overtook them; for they had not gone many leagues before a dreadful tempest arose, which burst their cables; down came their mast, crushing the skull of the pilot in its fall; off he fell from the stern into the water, and the bark wanting his management drove along at the wind's mercy. Thunders roared, and terrible lightnings of Jove came down; first a bolt struck Eurylochus, then another, and then another, till all the crew were killed, and their bodies swam about like sea-mews; and the ship was split in pieces: only Ulysses survived; and he had no hope of safety but in tying himself to the mast, where he sat riding upon the waves, like one that in no extremity would yield to fortune. Nine days was he floating about with all the motions of the sea, with no other support than the slender mast under him, till the tenth night cast him, all spent and weary with toil, upon the friendly shores of the island Ogygia.

Chapter 4

The island of Calypso. Immortality refused.

HENCEFORTH the adventures of the single Ulysses must be pursued. Of all those faithful partakers of his toil, who with him left Asia, laden with the spoils of Troy, now not one remains, but all a prey to the remorseless waves, and food for some great fish; their gallant navy reduced to one ship, and that finally swallowed up and lost. Where now are all their anxious thoughts of home? that perseverance with which they went through the severest sufferings and the hardest labours to which poor seafarers were ever exposed, that their toils at last might be crowned with the sight of their native shores and wives at Ithaca! Ulysses is now in the isle Ogygia, called the Delightful Island. The poor shipwrecked chief, the slave of all the elements, is once again raised by the caprice of fortune into a shadow of prosperity. He that was cast naked upon the shore, bereft of all his companions, has now a goddess to attend upon him, and his companions are the nymphs which never die.--Who has not heard of Calypso? her grove crowned with alders and poplars? her grotto, against which the luxuriant vine laid forth his purple grapes? her ever new delights, crystal fountains, running brooks, meadows flowering with sweet balm-gentle and with violet: blue violets which like veins enamelled the smooth breasts of each fragrant mead! It were useless to describe over again what has been so well told already; or to relate those soft arts of courtship which the goddess used to detain Ulysses; the same in kind which she afterwards practised upon his less wary son, whom Minerva, in the shape of Mentor, hardly preserved from her snares, when they came to the Delightful Island together in search of the scarce departed Ulysses.

A memorable example of married love, and a worthy instance how dear to every good man his country is, was exhibited by Ulysses. If Circe loved him sincerely, Calypso loves him with tenfold more warmth and passion. She can deny him nothing, but his departure; she offers him everything, even to a participation of her immortality; if he will stay and share in her pleasures, he shall never die. But death with glory has greater charms for a mind heroic, than a life that shall never die, with shame; and when he pledged his vows to his Penelope, he reserved no stipulation that he would forsake her whenever a goddess should think him worthy of her. They had sworn to live and grow old together; and he would not survive her if he could, nor meanly share in immortality itself, from which she was excluded.

These thoughts kept him pensive and melancholy in the midst of pleasure. His heart was on the seas, making voyages to Ithaca. Twelve months had worn away, when Minerva from heaven saw her favourite, how he sat still pining on the sea shores (his daily custom), wishing for a ship to carry him home. She (who is wisdom itself) was indignant that so wise and brave a man as Ulysses should be held in effeminate bondage by an unworthy goddess; and at her request, her father Jove ordered Mercury to go down to the earth to command Calypso to dismiss her guest. The divine messenger tied fast to his feet his winged shoes, which bear him over land and seas, and took in his hand his golden rod, the ensign of his authority. Then wheeling in many an airy round, he stayed not till he alighted on the firm top of the mountain Pieria. Thence he fetched a second circuit over the seas, kissing the waves in his flight with his feet, as light as any sea-mew fishing dips her wings, till he touched the isle Ogygia, and soared up from the blue sea to the grotto of the goddess, to whom his errand was ordained.

His message struck a horror, checked by love, through all the faculties of Calypso. She replied to it incensed, "You gods are insatiate, past all that live, in all things which you affect; which makes you so envious and grudging. It afflicts you to the heart, when any goddess seeks the love of a mortal man in marriage, though you yourselves without scruple link yourselves to women of the earth. And now you envy me the possession of a wretched man, whom tempests have cast upon my shores, making him lawfully mine; whose ship Jove rent in pieces with his hot thunderbolts, killing all his friends. Him I have preserved, loved, nourished, made him mine by protection, by every tie of gratitude mine; have vowed to make him deathless like myself; him you will take from me. But I know your power, and that it is vain for me to resist. Tell your king that I obey his mandates."

With an ill grace Calypso promised to fulfil the commands of Jove; and, Mercury departing, she went to find Ulysses, where he sat outside the grotto, not knowing of the heavenly message, drowned in discontent, not seeing any human probability of his ever returning home.

She said to him, "Unhappy man, no longer afflict yourself with pining after your country, but build you a ship, with which you may return home; since it is the will of the gods; who doubtless, as they art greater in power than I, are greater in skill, and best can tell what is fittest for man. But I call the gods, and my inward conscience, to witness, that I had no thought but what stood with thy safety, nor would have done or counselled anything against thy good. I persuaded thee to nothing which should not have followed myself in thy extremity; for my mind is innocent and simple. O, if thou knewest what dreadful sufferings thou must yet endure, before ever thou reachest thy native land, thou wouldst not esteem so hardly of a goddess's offer to share her immortality with thee; nor, for a few years' enjoyment of a perishing Penelope, refuse an imperishable and never-dying life with Calypso."

He replied, "Ever-honoured, great Calypso, let it not displease thee, that I, a mortal man, desire to see and converse again with a wife that is mortal: human objects are best fitted to human infirmities. I well know how far in wisdom, in feature, in stature, proportion, beauty, in all the gifts of the mind, thou exceedest my Penelope: she a mortal, and subject to decay; thou immortal, ever growing, yet never old; yet in her sight all my desires terminate, all my wishes; in the sight of her, and of my country earth. If any god, envious of my return, shall lay his dreadful hand upon me as I pass the seas, I submit; for the same powers have given me a mind not to sink under oppression. In wars and waves my sufferings have not been small."

She heard his pleaded reasons, and of force she must assent; so to her nymphs she gave in charge from her sacred woods to cut down timber, to make Ulysses a ship. They obeyed, though in a work unsuitable to their soft fingers, yet to obedience no sacrifice is hard: and Ulysses busily bestirred himself, labouring far more hard than they, as was fitting, till twenty tall trees, driest and fittest for timber, were felled. Then like a skilful shipwright, he fell to joining the planks, using the plane, the axe, and the auger, with such expedition, that in four days' time a ship was made, complete with all her decks, hatches, sideboards, yards. Calypso added linen for the sails, and tackling; and when she was finished, she was a goodly vessel for a man to sail in alone, or in company, over the wide sea. By the fifth morning she was launched; and Ulysses, furnished with store of provisions, rich garments, and gold and silver, given him by Calypso, took a last leave of her, and of her nymphs, and of the isle Ogygia, which had so befriended him.

Chapter 5

The tempest. The sea-bird's gift. The escape by swimming. The sleep in the woods.

AT the stern of his solitary ship Ulysses sat, and steered right artfully. No sleep could seize his eyelids. He beheld the Pleiads, the Bear which is by some called the Wain, that moves round about Orion, and keeps still above the ocean, and the slow-setting sign Bootes, which some name the Waggoner. Seventeen days he held his course, and on the eighteenth the coast of Phæacia was in sight. The figure of the land, as seen from the sea, was pretty and circular, and looked something like a shield.

Neptune, returning from visiting his favourite Æthiopians, from the mountains of the Solymi, descried Ulysses ploughing the waves, his domain. The sight of the man he so much hated for Polyphemus' sake, his son, whose eye Ulysses had put out, set the god's heart on fire, and snatching into his hand his horrid sea-sceptre, the trident of his power, he smote the air and the sea, and conjured up all his black storms, calling down night from the cope of heaven, and taking the earth into the sea, as it seemed, with clouds, through the darkness and indistinctness which prevailed, the billows rolling up before the fury of all the winds, that contended together in their mighty sport.

Then the knees of Ulysses bent with fear, and then all his spirit was spent, and he wished that he had been among the number of his countrymen who fell before Troy, and had their funerals celebrated by all the Greeks, rather than to perish thus, where no man could mourn him or know him.

As he thought these melancholy thoughts, a huge wave took him and washed him overboard, ship and all upset amidst the billows; he struggling afar off, clinging to her stern broken off, which he yet held; her mast cracking in two with the fury of that gust of mixed winds that struck it; sails and sail-yards fell into the deep, and he himself was long drowned under water, nor could get his head above, wave so met with wave, as if they strove which should depress him most; and the gorgeous garments given him by Calypso clung about him, and hindered his swimming. Yet neither for this, nor for the overthrow of his ship, nor his own perilous condition, would he give up his drenched vessel; but, wrestling with Neptune, got at length hold of her again, and then sat in her hulk, insulting over death, which he had escaped, and the salt waves which he gave the sea again to give to other men. His ship, striving to live, floated at random, cuffed from wave to wave, hurled to and fro by all the winds: now Boreas tossed it to Notus, Notus passed it to Eurus, and Eurus to the west wind, who kept up the horrid tennis.

Them in their mad sport Ino Leucothea beheld; Ino Leucothea, now a sea-goddess, but once a mortal and the daughter of Cadmus; she with pity beheld Ulysses the mark of their fierce contention, and rising from the waves alighted on the ship, in shape like to the sea-bird which is called a cormorant, and in her beak she held a wonderful girdle made of sea-weeds which grow at the bottom of the ocean, which she dropped at his feet. And the bird spake to Ulysses, and counselled him not to trust any more to that fatal vessel against which god Neptune had levelled his furious wrath, nor to those ill-befriending garments which Calypso had given him, but to quit both it and them, and trust for his safety to swimming. "And here," said the seeming bird, "take this girdle and tie about your middle, which has virtue to protect the wearer at sea, and you shall safely reach the shore; but when you have landed, cast it far from you back into the sea." He did as the sea-bird instructed him, he stripped himself naked, and fastening the wondrous girdle about his middle, cast himself into the seas to swim. The bird dived past his sight into the fathomless abyss of the ocean.

Two days and two nights he spent in struggling with the waves, though sore buffeted and almost spent, never giving up himself for lost, such confidence he had in that charm which he wore about his middle, and in the words of that divine bird. But the third morning the winds grew calm, and all the heavens were clear. Then he saw himself nigh land, which he knew to be the coast of the Phæacians, a people good to strangers, and abounding in ships, by whose favour he doubted not that he should soon obtain a passage to his own country. And such joy he conceived in his heart, as good sons have that esteem their father's life dear, when long sickness has held him down to his bed and wasted his body, and they see at length health return to the old man, with restored strength and spirits, in reward of their many prayers to the gods for his safety: so precious was the prospect of home-return to Ulysses, that he might restore health to his country (his better parent), that had long languished as full of distempers in his absence. And then for his own safety's sake he had joy to see the shores, the woods, so nigh and within his grasp as they seemed, and he laboured with all the might of hands and feet to reach with swimming that nigh-seeming land.

But when he approached near, a horrid sound of a huge sea beating against rocks informed him that here was no place for landing, nor any harbour for man's resort; but through the weeds and the foam which the sea belched up against the land he could dimly discover the rugged shore all bristled with flints, and all that part of the coast one impending rock that seemed impossible to climb, and the water all about so deep, that not a sand was there for any tired foot to rest upon, and every moment he feared lest some wave more cruel than the rest should crush him against a cliff, rendering worse than vain all his landing. And should he swim to seek a more commodious haven farther on, he was fearful lest, weak and spent as he was, the winds would force him back a long way off into the main, where the terrible god Neptune, for wrath that he had so nearly escaped his power, having gotten him again into his domain, would send out some great whale (of which those seas breed a horrid number) to swallow him up alive; with such malignity he still pursued him.

While these thoughts distracted him with diversity of dangers, one bigger wave drove against a sharp rock his naked body, which it gashed and tore, and wanted little of breaking all his bones, so rude was the shock. But in this extremity she prompted him that never failed him at need. Minerva (who is wisdom itself) put it into his thoughts no longer to keep swimming off and on, as one dallying with danger, but bodily to force the shore that threatened him, and to hug the rock that had torn him so rudely; which with both hands he clasped, wrestling with extremity, till the rage of that billow which had driven him upon it was past. But then again the rock drove back that wave so furiously, that it reft him of his hold, sucking him with it in its return, and the sharp rock (his cruel friend) to which he clinged for succour, rent the flesh so sore from his hands in parting, that he fell off, and could sustain no longer. Quite under water he fell, and past the help of fate, there had the hapless Ulysses lost all portion that he had in this life, if Minerva had not prompted his wisdom in that peril to essay another course, and to explore some other shelter, ceasing to attempt that landing-place.

She guided his wearied and nigh-exhausted limbs to the mouth of the fair river Calliroe, which not far from thence disbursed its watery tribute to the ocean. Here the shores were easy and accessible, and the rocks, which rather adorned than defended its banks, so smooth, that they seemed polished of purpose to invite the landing of our sea-wanderer, and to atone for the uncourteous treatment which those less hospitable cliffs had afforded him. And the god of the river, as if in pity, stayed his current and smoothed his waters, to make his landing more easy; for sacred to the ever-living deities of the fresh waters, be they mountain-stream, river, or lake, is the cry of erring mortals that seek their aid, by reason that being inland-bred they partake more of the gentle humanities of our nature than those marine deities, whom Neptune trains up in tempests in the unpitying recesses of his salt abyss.

So by the favour of the river's god Ulysses crept to land half-drowned; both his knees faltering, his strong hands falling down through weakness from the excessive toils he had endured, his cheek and nostrils flowing with froth of the sea-brine, much of which he had swallowed in that conflict, voice and breath spent, down he sank as in death. Dead weary he was. It seemed that the sea had soaked through his heart, and the pains he felt in all his veins were little less than those which one feels that has endured the torture of the rack. But when his spirits came a little to themselves, and his recollection by degrees began to return, he rose up, and unloosing from his waist the girdle of charm which that divine bird had given him, and remembering the charge which he had received with it, he flung it far from him into the river. Back it swam with the course of the ebbing stream till it reached the sea, where the fair hands of Ino Leucothea received it, to keep it as a pledge of safety to any future shipwrecked mariner, that like Ulysses should wander in those perilous waves.

Then he kissed the humble earth in token of safety; and on he went by the side of that pleasant river, till he came where a thicker shade of rushes that grew on its banks seemed to point out the place where he might rest his sea-wearied limbs. And here a fresh perplexity divided his mind, whether he should pass the night, which was coming on, in that place, where, though he feared no other enemies, the damps and frosts of the chill sea-air in that exposed situation might be death to him in his weak state; or whether he had better climb the next hill, and pierce the depth of some shady wood, in which he might find a warm and sheltered though insecure repose, subject to the approach of any wild beast that roamed that way. Best did this last course appear to him, though with some danger, as that which was more honourable and savoured more of strife and self-exertion, than to perish without a struggle the passive victim of cold and the elements.

So he bent his course to the nearest woods, where, entering in, he found a thicket, mostly of wild olives and such low trees, yet growing so intertwined and knit together, that the moist wind had not leave to play through their branches, nor the sun's scorching beams to pierce their recesses, nor any shower to beat through, they grew so thick, and as it were folded each in the other. Here creeping in, he made his bed of the leaves which were beginning to fall, of which was such abundance that two or three men might have spread them ample coverings, such as might shield them from the winter's rage, though the air breathed steel and blew as it would burst. Here creeping in, he heaped up store of leaves all about him, as a man would billets upon a winter fire, and lay down in the midst. Rich seed of virtue lying hid in poor leaves! Here Minerva soon gave him sound sleep; and here all his long toils past seemed to be concluded and shut up within the little sphere of his refreshed and closed eyelids.

Chapter 6

The princess Nausicaa. The washing. The game with the ball. The Court of Phæacia and king Alcinous.

MEANTIME Minerva, designing an interview between the king's daughter of that country and Ulysses when he should awake, went by night to the palace of king Alcinous, and stood at the bedside of the princess Nausicaa in the shape of one of her favourite attendants, and thus addressed the sleeping princess:

"Nausicaa, why do you lie sleeping here, and never bestow a thought upon your bridal ornaments, of which you have many and beautiful, laid up in your wardrobe against the day of your marriage, which cannot be far distant, when you shall have need of all, not only to deck your own person, but to give away in presents to the virgins that honouring you shall attend you to the temple? Your reputation stands much upon the timely care of these things; these things are they which fill father and reverend mother with delight. Let us arise betimes to wash your fair vestments of linen and silks in the river; and request your sire to lend you mules and a coach, for your wardrobe is heavy, and the place where we must wash is distant, and besides it fits not a great princess like you to go so far on foot."

So saying she went away, and Nausicaa awoke, full of pleasing thoughts of her marriage, which the dream had told her was not far distant; and as soon as it was dawn, she arose and dressed herself and went to find her parents.

The queen her mother was already up, and seated among her maids, spinning at her wheel, as the fashion was in those primitive times, when great ladies did not disdain housewifery; and the king her father was preparing to go abroad at that early hour to council with his grave senate.

"My father," she said, "will you not order mules and a coach to be got ready, that I may go and wash, I and my maids, at the cisterns that stand without the city?"

"What washing does my daughter speak of?" said Alcinous.

"Mine and my brothers' garments," she replied, "that have contracted soil by this time with lying by so long in the wardrobe. Five sons have you, that are my brothers; two of them are married, and three are bachelors; these last it concerns to have their garments neat and unsoiled; it may advance their fortunes in marriage; and who but me their sister should have a care of these things? You yourself, my father, have need of the whitest apparel, when you go, as now, to the council."

She used this plea, modestly dissembling her care of her own nuptials to her father; who was not displeased at this instance of his daughter's discretion; for a seasonable care about marriage may be permitted to a young maiden, provided it be accompanied with modesty and dutiful submission to her parents in the choice of her future husband. And there was no fear of Nausicaa choosing wrongly or improperly, for she was as wise as she was beautiful, and the best in all Phæacia were suitors to her for her love. So Alcinous readily gave consent that she should go, ordering mules and a coach to be prepared. And Nausicaa brought from her chamber all her vestments, and laid them up in the coach, and her mother placed bread and wine in the coach. Nausicaa, making her maids get up into the coach with her, lashed the mules, till they brought her to the cisterns which stood a little on the outside of the town, and were supplied with water from the river Calliroe.

There her attendants unyoked the mules, took out the clothes, and steeped them in the cisterns, washing them in several waters, and afterwards treading them clean with their feet, venturing wagers who should have done soonest and cleanest, and using many pretty pastimes to beguile their labour as young maids use, while the princess looked on. When they had laid their clothes to dry, they fell to playing again, and Nausicaa joined them in a game with the ball, which is used in that country; which is performed by tossing the ball from hand to hand with great expedition, she who begins the pastime singing a song. It chanced that the princess, whose turn it became to toss the ball, sent it so far from its mark, that it fell beyond into one of the cisterns of the river; at which the whole company, in merry consternation, set up a shriek so loud as waked the sleeping Ulysses, who was taking his rest after his long toils, in the woods not far distant from the place where these young maids had come to wash.

At the sound of female voices Ulysses crept forth from his retirement, making himself a covering with boughs and leaves as well as he could to shroud his nakedness. The sudden appearance of his weather-beaten and almost naked form so frightened the maidens, that they scudded away into the woods and all about to hide themselves; only Minerva (who had brought about this interview to admirable purposes, by seemingly accidental means) put courage into the breast of Nausicaa, and she stayed where she was, and resolved to know what manner of man he was, and what was the occasion of his strange coming to them.

He, not venturing (for delicacy) to approach and clasp her knees, as suppliants should, but standing far off, addressed this speech to the young princess:

'Before I presume rudely to press my petitions, I should first ask whether I am addressing a mortal woman, or one of the goddesses. If a goddess, you seem to me to be likest to Diana, the chaste huntress, the daughter of Jove. Like hers are your lineaments, your stature, your features, and air divine."

She making answer that she was no goddess, but a mortal maid, he continued:

"If a woman, thrice blessed are both the authors of your birth, thrice blessed are your brothers, who even to rapture must have joy in your perfections, to see you grown so like a young tree, and so graceful. But most blessed of all that breathe is he that has the gift to engage your young neck in the yoke of marriage. I never saw that man that was worthy of you. I never saw man or woman that at all parts equalled you. Lately at Delos (where I touched) I saw a young palm which grew beside Apollo's temple; it exceeded all the trees which ever I beheld for straightness and beauty: I can compare you only to that. A stupor past admiration strikes me, joined with fear, which keeps me back from approaching you, to embrace your knees. Nor is it strange; for one of freshest and firmest spirit would falter, approaching near to so bright an object; but I am one whom a cruel habit of calamity has prepared to receive strong impressions. Twenty days the unrelenting seas have tossed me up and down coming from Ogygia, and at length cast me shipwrecked last night upon your coast. I have seen no man or woman since I landed but yourself. All that I crave is clothes, which you may spare me, and to be shown the way to some neighbouring town. The gods who have care of strangers, will requite you for these courtesies."

She admiring to hear such complimentary words proceed out of the mouth of one whose outside looked so rough and unpromising, made answer: "Stranger, I discern neither sloth nor folly in you, and yet I see that you are poor and wretched; from which I gather that neither wisdom nor industry can secure felicity; only Jove bestows it upon whomsoever he pleases. He perhaps has reduced you to this plight. However, since your wanderings have brought you so near to our city, it lies in our duty to supply your wants. Clothes and what else a human hand should give to one so suppliant, and so tamed with calamity, you shall not want. We will show you our city, and tell you the name of our people. This is the land of the Phæacians, of which my father Alcinous is king."

Then calling her attendants, who had dispersed on the first sight of Ulysses, she rebuked them for their fear, and said, "This man is no Cyclop, nor monster of sea or land, that you should fear him; but he seems manly, staid, and discreet, and though decayed in his outward appearance, yet he has the mind's riches,--wit and fortitude, in abundance. Show him the cisterns where he may wash him from the sea-weeds and foam that hang about him, and let him have garments that fit him out of those which we have brought with us to the cisterns."

Ulysses retiring a little out of sight, cleansed him in the cisterns from the soil and impurities with which the rocks and waves had covered all his body, and clothing himself with befitting raiment, which the princess's attendants had given him, he presented himself in more worthy shape to Nausicaa. She admired to see what a comely personage he was, now he was dressed in all parts; she thought him some king or hero, and secretly wished that the gods would be pleased to give her such a husband.

Then causing her attendants to yoke her mules, and lay up the vestments, which the sun's heat had sufficiently dried, in the coach, she ascended with her maids, and drove off to the palace; bidding Ulysses, as she departed, keep an eye upon the coach, and to follow it on foot at some distance: which she did, because if she had suffered him to have ridden in the coach with her, it might have subjected her to some misconstructions of the common people. So discreet and attentive to appearance in all her actions was this admirable princess.

Ulysses, as he entered the city, wondered to see its magnificence, its markets, buildings, temples; its walls and rampires; its trade, and resort of men; its harbours for shipping, which is the strength of the Phæacian state. But when he approached the palace, and beheld its riches, the proportion of its architecture, its avenues, gardens, statues, fountains, he stood rapt in admiration, and almost forgot his own condition in surveying the flourishing estate of others. But recollecting himself he passed on boldly into the inner apartment, where the king and queen were sitting at dinner with their peers; Nausicaa having prepared them for his approach.

To them, humbly kneeling, he made it his request, that since fortune had cast him naked upon their shores, they would take him into their protection, and grant him a conveyance by one of the ships, of which their great Phæacian state had such good store, to carry him to his own country. Having delivered his request, to grace it with more humility, he went and sat himself down upon the hearth among the ashes, as the custom was in those days when any would make a petition to the throne.

He seemed a petitioner of so great state and of so superior a deportment, that Alcinous himself arose to do him honour; and, causing him to leave that abject station which he had assumed, placed him next to his throne, upon a chair of state, and thus he spake to his peers:

"Lords and counsellors of Phæacia, ye see this man, who he is we know not, that is come to us in the guise of a petitioner: he seems no mean one; but whoever he is, it is fit, since the gods have cast him upon our protection, that we grant him the rites of hospitality while he stays with us, and at his departure a ship well manned to convey so worthy a personage as he seems to be, in a manner suitable to his rank, to his own country."

This counsel the peers with one consent approved; and wine and meat being set before Ulysses, he ate and drank, and gave the gods thanks who had stirred up the royal bounty of Alcinous to aid him in that extremity. But not as yet did he reveal to the king and queen who he was, or whence he had come; only in brief terms he related his being cast upon their shores, his sleep in the woods, and his meeting with the princess Nausicaa; whose generosity, mingled with discretion, filled her parents with delight, as Ulysses in eloquent phrases adorned and commended her virtues. But Alcinous, humanely considering that the troubles which his guest had undergone required rest, as well as refreshment by food, dismissed him early in the evening to his chamber; where in a magnificent apartment Ulysses found a smoother bed, but not a sounder repose, than he had enjoyed the night before, sleeping upon leaves which he had scraped together in his necessity.

Chapter 7

The songs of Demodocus. The convoy home. The mariners transformed to stone. The young shepherd.

WHEN it was day-light, Alcinous caused it to be proclaimed by the heralds about the town that there was come to the palace a stranger, shipwrecked on their coast, that in mien and person resembled a god; and inviting all the chief people of the city to come and do honour to the stranger.

The palace was quickly filled with guests, old and young, for whose cheer, and to grace Ulysses more, Alcinous made a kingly feast, with banquetings and music. Then Ulysses being seated at a table next the king and queen, in all men's view, after they had feasted, Alcinous ordered Demodocus, the court-singer, to be called to sing some song of the deeds of heroes, to charm the ear of his guest. Demodocus came and reached his harp, where it hung between two pillars of silver; and then the blind singer, to whom, in recompense of his lost sight, the muses had given an inward discernment, a soul and a voice to excite the hearts of men and gods to delight, began in grave and solemn strains to sing the glories of men highliest famed. He chose a poem, whose subject was the stern strife stirred up between Ulysses and great Achilles, as at a banquet sacred to the gods in dreadful language they expressed their difference; while Agamemnon sat rejoiced in soul to hear those Grecians jar; for the oracle in Pytho had told him, that the period of their wars in Troy should then be, when the kings of Greece, anxious to arrive at the wished conclusion, should fall to strife, and contend which must end the war, force or stratagem.

This brave contention he expressed so to the life, in the very words which they both used in the quarrel, as brought tears into the eyes of Ulysses at the remembrance of past passages of his life, and he held his large purple weed before his face to conceal it. Then craving a cup of wine, he poured it out in secret libation to the gods, who had put into the mind of Demodocus unknowingly to do him so much honour. But when the moving poet began to tell of other occurrences where Ulysses had been present, the memory of his brave followers who had been with him in all difficulties, now swallowed up and lost in the ocean, and of those kings that had fought with him at Troy, some of whom were dead, some exiles like himself, forced itself so strongly upon his mind, that forgetful where he was, he sobbed outright with passion; which yet he restrained, but not so cunningly but Alcinous perceived it, and without taking notice of it to Ulysses, privately gave signs that Demodocus should cease from his singing.

Next followed dancing in the Phæacian fashion, when they would show respect to their guests; which was succeeded by trials of skill, games of strength, running, racing, hurling of the quoit, mock fights, hurling of the javelin, shooting with the bow; in some of which Ulysses modestly challenging his entertainers, performed such feats of strength and prowess as gave the admiring Phæacians fresh reason to imagine that he was either some god, or hero of the race of the gods.

These solemn shows and pageants in honour of his guest, king Alcinous continued for the space of many days, as if he could never be weary of showing courtesies to so worthy a stranger. In all this time he never asked him his name, nor sought to know more of him than he of his own accord disclosed; till on a day as they were seated feasting, after the feast was ended, Demodocus being called, as was the custom, to sing some grave matter, sang how Ulysses, on that night when Troy was fired, made dreadful proof of his valour, maintaining singly a combat against the whole household of Deiphobus; which made Ulysses even pity his own slaughterous deeds, and feel touches of remorse; and in imagination he underwent some part of death's horrors, that with the strong conceit, tears (the true interpreters of unutterable emotion) stood in his eyes.

Which king Alcinous noting, and that this was now the second time that he had perceived him to be moved at the mention of events touching the Trojan wars, he took occasion to ask whether his guest had lost any friend or kinsman at Troy, that Demodocus' singing had brought into his mind. Then Ulysses, drying the tears with his cloak, and observing that the eyes of all the company were upon him, desirous to give them satisfaction in what he could, and thinking this a fit time to reveal his true name and destination, spake as follows:

"The courtesies which ye all have shown me and in particular yourself and princely daughter, O king Alcinous, demand from me that I should no longer keep you in ignorance of what or who I am; for to reserve any secret from you, who have with such openness of friendship embraced my love, would argue either a pusillanimous or an ungrateful mind in me. Know then that I am that *Ulysses*, of whom I perceive ye have heard something; who heretofore have filled the world with the renown of my policies. I am he by whose counsels, if Fame is to be believed at all, more than by the united valour of all the Grecians, Troy fell. I am that unhappy man whom the heavens and angry gods have conspired to keep an exile on the seas, wandering to seek my home, which still flies from me. The land which I am in quest of is Ithaca; in whose ports some ship belonging to your navigation-famed Phæacian state may haply at some time have found a refuge from tempests. If ever you have experienced such kindness, requite it now, by granting to me, who am the king of that land, a passport to that land."

Admiration seized all the court of Alcinous to behold in their presence one of the number of those heroes who fought at Troy, whose divine story had been made known to them by songs and poems; but of the truth they had little known, or rather they had hitherto accounted those heroic exploits as fictions and exaggerations of poets; but having seen and made proof of the real Ulysses, they began to take those supposed inventions to be real verities, and the tale of Troy to be as true as it was delightful.

Then king Alcinous made answer: "Thrice fortunate ought we to esteem our lot, in having seen and conversed with a man of whom report hath spoken so loudly, but, as it seems, nothing beyond the truth. Though we could desire no felicity greater than to have you always among us, renowned Ulysses, yet your desire having been expressed so often and so deeply to return home, we can deny you nothing, though to our own loss. Our kingdom of Phæacia, as you know, is chiefly rich in shipping. In all parts of the world, where there are navigable seas, or ships can pass, our vessels will be found. You cannot name a coast to which they do not resort. Every rock and deep quick-sand is known to them, that lurks in the vast deep. They pass a bird in flight; and with such unerring certainty they make to their destination, that some have said they have no need of pilot or rudder, but that they move instinctively, self-directed, and know the minds of their voyagers. Thus much, that you may not fear to trust yourself in one of our Phæacian ships. To-morrow, if you please, you shall launch forth. To-day spend with us in feasting, who never can do enough when the gods send such visitors."

Ulysses acknowledged king Alcinous' bounty; and while these two royal personages stood interchanging courteous expressions, the heart of the princess Nausicaa was overcome. She had been gazing attentively upon her father's guest, as he delivered his speech; but when he came to that part where he declared himself to be Ulysses, she blessed herself and her fortune that in relieving a poor shipwrecked mariner, as he seemed no better, she had conferred a kindness on so divine a hero as he proved; and scarce waiting till her father had done speaking, with a cheerful countenance she addressed Ulysses, bidding him be cheerful, and when he returned home, as by her father's means she trusted he would shortly, sometimes to remember to whom he owed his life, and who met him in the woods by the river Calliroe.

"Fair flower of Phæacia," he replied, " so may all the gods bless me with the strife of joys in that desired day, whenever I shall see it, as I shall always acknowledge to be indebted to your fair hand for the gift of life which I enjoy, and all the blessings which shall follow upon my home-return. The gods give thee, Nausicaa, a princely husband; and from you two spring blessings to this state." So prayed Ulysses, his heart overflowing with admiration and grateful recollections of king Alcinous' daughter.

Then at the king's request he gave them a brief relation of all the adventures that had befallen him since he launched forth from Troy; during which the princess Nausicaa took great delight (as ladies are commonly taken with these kind of travellers' stories) to hear of the monster Polyphemus, of the men that devour each other in Læstrygonia, of the enchantress Circe, of Scylla, and the rest; to which she listened with a breathless attention, letting fall a shower of tears from her fair eyes every now and then, when Ulysses told of some more than usual distressful passage in his travels. And all the rest of his auditors, if they had before entertained a high respect for their guest, now felt their veneration increased tenfold, when they learnt from his own mouth what perils, what sufferings, what endurance, of evils beyond man's strength to support, this much-sustaining, almost heavenly man, by the greatness of his mind, and by his invincible courage, had struggled through.

The night was far spent before Ulysses had ended his narrative, and with wishful glances he cast his eyes towards the eastern parts, which the sun had begun to flecker with his first red; for on the morrow Alcinous had promised that a bark should be in readiness to convoy him to Ithaca.

In the morning a vessel well manned and appointed was waiting for him; into which the king and queen heaped presents of gold and silver, massy plate, apparel, armour, and whatsoever things of cost or rarity they judged would be most acceptable to their guest. And the sails being set, Ulysses, embarking with expressions of regret, took his leave of his royal entertainers, of the fair princess (who had been his first friend), and of the peers of Phæacia; who crowding down to the beach to have the last sight of their illustrious visitant, beheld the gallant ship with all her canvas spread, bounding and curveting over the waves, like a horse proud of his rider; or as if she knew that in her capacious waist's rich freightage she bore Ulysses.

He whose life past had been a series of disquiets, in seas among rude waves, in battles amongst ruder foes, now slept securely, forgetting all; his eye-lids bound in such deep sleep, as only yielded to death; and when they reached the nearest Ithacan port by the next morning, he was still asleep. The mariners not willing to awake him, landed him softly, and laid him in a cave at the foot of an olive-tree, which made a shady recess in that narrow harbour, the haunt of almost none but the sea-nymphs, which are called Naiads; few ships before this Phæacian vessel having put into that haven, by reason of the difficulty and narrowness of the entrance. Here leaving him asleep, and disposing in safe places near him the presents with which king Alcinous had dismissed him, they departed for Phæacia, where these wretched mariners never again set foot; but just as they arrived, and thought to salute their country earth, in sight of their city's turrets, and in open view of their friends who from the harbour with shouts greeted their return, their vessel and all the mariners which were in her were turned to stone, and stood transformed and fixed in sight of the whole Phæacian city, where it yet stands, by Neptune's vindictive wrath; who resented thus highly the contempt which those Phæacians had shown in convoying home a man whom the god had destined to destruction. Whence it comes to pass that all the Phæacians at this day will at no price be induced to lend their ships to strangers, or to become carriers for other nations; so highly do they still dread the displeasure of the sea-god, while they see that terrible monument ever in sight.

When Ulysses awoke, which was not till some time after the mariners had departed, he did not at first know his country again, either that long absence had made it strange, or that Minerva (which was more likely) had cast a cloud about his eyes, that he should have greater pleasure here-after in discovering his mistake. But like a man suddenly awaking in some desert isle, to which his sea-mates have transported him in his sleep, he looked around, and discerning no known objects, he cast his hands to heaven for pity, and complained of those ruthless men who had beguiled him with a promise of conveying him home to his country, and perfidiously left him to perish in an unknown land. But then the rich presents of gold and silver given him by Alcinous, which he saw carefully laid up in secure places near him, staggered him; which seemed not like the act of wrongful or unjust men, such as turn pirates for gain, or land helpless passengers in remote coasts to possess themselves of their goods.

While he remained in this suspence, there came up to him a young shepherd, clad in the finer sort of apparel, such as kings' sons wore in those days when princes did not disdain to tend sheep, who accosting him, was saluted again by Ulysses, who asked him what country that was, on which he had been just landed, and whether it were a part of a continent or an island. The young shepherd made show of wonder, to hear any one ask the name of that land; as country people are apt to esteem those for mainly ignorant and barbarous who do not know the names of places which are familiar to *them*, though perhaps they who ask have had no opportunities of knowing, and may have come from far countries.

"I had thought," said he, "that all people knew our land. It is rocky and barren, to be sure; but well enough. It feeds a goat or an ox well; it is not wanting either in wine or in wheat; it has good springs of water, some fair rivers, and wood enough, as you may see. It is called Ithaca."

Ulysses was joyed enough to find himself in his own country; but so prudently he carried his joy, that dissembling his true name and quality, he pretended to the shepherd that he was only some foreigner who by stress of weather had put into that port; and framed on the sudden a story to make it plausible, how he had come from Crete in a ship of Phæacia; when the young shepherd laughing, and taking Ulysses' hand in both his, said to him, "He must be cunning, I find, who thinks to overreach you. What, cannot you quit your wiles and your subtleties, now that you are in a state of security? must the first word with which you salute your native earth be an untruth? and think you that you are unknown?"

Ulysses looked again; and he saw, not a shepherd, but a beautiful woman, whom he immediately knew to be the goddess Minerva, that in the wars of Troy had frequently vouchsafed her sight to him; and had been with him since in perils, saving him unseen.

"Let not my ignorance offend thee, great Minerva" he cried, "or move thy displeasure, that in that shape I knew thee not; since the skill of discerning of the deities is not attainable by wit or study, but hard to be hit by the wisest of mortals. To know thee truly through all thy changes is only given to those whom thou art pleased to grace. To all men thou takest all likenesses. All men in their wits think that they know thee, and that they have thee. Thou art wisdom itself. But a semblance of thee, which is false wisdom, often is taken for thee; so thy counterfeit views appear to many, but thy true presence to few: those are they which, loving thee above all, are inspired with light from thee to know thee. But this I surely know, that all the time the sons of Greece waged war against Troy, I was sundry times graced with thy appearance; but since, I have never been able to set eyes upon thee till now; but have wandered at my own discretion, to myself a blind guide, erring up and down the world, wanting thee."

Then Minerva cleared his eyes, and he knew the ground on which he stood to be Ithaca, and that cave to be the same which the people of Ithaca had in former times made sacred to the sea-nymphs, and where he himself had done sacrifices to them a thousand times; and full in his view stood Mount Nerytus with all its woods, so that now he knew for a certainty that he was arrived in his own country, and with the delight which he felt he could not forbear stooping down and kissing the soil.

Chapter 8

The change from a king to a beggar. Eumæus and the herdsmen. Telemachus.

NOT long did Minerva suffer him to indulge vain transports, but briefly recounting to him the events which had taken place in Ithaca during his absence, she showed him that his way to his wife and throne did not lie so open, but that before he was reinstated in the secure possession of them, he must encounter many difficulties. His palace, wanting its king, was become a resort of insolent and imperious men, the chief nobility of Ithaca and of the neighbouring isles, who, in the confidence of Ulysses being dead, came as suitors to Penelope. The queen (it was true) continued single, but was little better than a state-prisoner in the power of these men, who under a pretence of waiting her decision, occupied the king's house, rather as owners than guests, lording and domineering at their pleasure, profaning the palace, and wasting the royal substance, with their feasts and mad iots. Moreover the goddess told him how, fearing the attempts of these lawless men upon he person of his young son, Telemachus, she herself had put it into the heart of the prince to go and seek his father in far countries; how in the shape of Mentor she had borne him company in his long search; which, though failing, as she meant it should fail, in its first object, had yet had this effect, that through hardships he had learned endurance, through experience he had gathered wisdom, and wherever his footsteps had been he had left such memorials of hist worth, that he fame of Ulysses' son was already blown throughout the world. That it was now not many days since Telemachus had arrived in the island, to the great joy of the queen his mother, who had thought him dead, by reason of his long absence, and had begun to mourn for him with a grief equal to that which she endured for Ulysses; the goddess herself having so ordered the course of his adventures, that the time of his return should correspond with the return of Ulysses, that they might together concert measures how to repress the power and insolence of those wicked suitors. This the goddess told him; but of the particulars of his son's adventures, of his having been detained in the Delightful Island, which his father had so lately left, of Calypso and her nymphs, and the many strange occurrences which may be read with profit and delight in the history of the prince's adventures, she forbore to tell him as yet; as judging that he would hear them with greater pleasure from the lips of his son, when he should have him in an hour of stillness and safety, when their work should be done, and none of their enemies left alive to trouble him.

Then they sat down, the goddess and Ulysses, at the foot of a wild olive-tree, consulting how they might with safety bring about his restoration. And when Ulysses revolved in his mind how that his enemies were a multitude, and he single, he began to despond, and he said, "I shall die an ill death like Agamemnon; in the threshold of my own house I shall perish, like that unfortunate monarch, slain by some one of my wife's suitors." But then again calling to mind his ancient courage, he secretly wished that Minerva would but breathe such a spirit into his bosom as she enflamed him with in the day of Troy's destruction, that he might encounter with three hundred of those impudent suitors at once, and strew the pavements of his beautiful palace with their blood and brains.

And Minerva knew his thoughts, and she said, "I will be strongly with thee, if thou fail not to do thy part. And for a sign between us that I will perform my promise, and for a token on thy part of obedience, I must change thee, that thy person may not be known of men."

Then Ulysses bowed his head to receive the divine impression, and Minerva by her great power changed his person so that it might not be known. She changed him to appearance into a very old man, yet such a one as by his limbs and gait seemed to have been some considerable person in his time, and to retain yet some remains of his once prodigious strength. Also, instead of those rich robes in which king Alcinous had clothed him, she threw over his limbs such old and tattered rags as wandering beggars usually wear. A staff supported his steps, and a scrip hung to his back, such as travelling mendicants use, to hold the scraps which are given to them at rich men's doors. So from a king he became a beggar, as wise Tiresias had predicted to him in the shades.

To complete his humiliation, and to prove his obedience by suffering, she next directed him in this beggarly attire to go and present himself to his old herdsman Eumæus, who had the care of his swine and his cattle, and had been a faithful steward to him all the time of his absence. Then strictly charging Ulysses that he should reveal himself to no man but to his own son, whom she would send to him when she saw occasion, the goddess went her way.

The transformed Ulysses bent his course to the cottage of the herdsman, and entering in at the front court, the dogs, of which Eumæus kept many fierce ones for the protection of the cattle, flew with open mouths upon him, as those ignoble animals have oftentimes an antipathy to the sight of any thing like a beggar; and would have rent him in pieces with their teeth, if Ulysses had not had the prudence to let fall his staff, which had chiefly provoked their fury, and sat himself down in a careless fashion upon the ground; but for all that some serious hurt had certainly been done to him, so raging the dogs were, had not the herdsman, whom the barking of the dogs had fetched out of the house, with shouting and with throwing of stones repressed them.

He said, when he saw Ulysses, "Old father, how near you were to being torn in pieces by these rude dogs! I should never have forgiven myself, if through neglect of mine any hurt had happened to you. But heaven has given me so many cares to my portion, that I might well be excused for not attending to everything; while here I lie grieving and mourning for the absence of that majesty which once ruled here, and am forced to fatten his swine and his cattle for evil men, who hate him, and who wish his death; when he perhaps strays up and down the world, and has not wherewith to appease hunger, if indeed he yet lives (which is a question) and enjoys the cheerful light of the sun." This he said, little thinking that he of whom he spoke now stood before him, and that in that uncouth disguise and beggarly obscurity was present the hidden majesty of Ulysses.

Then he had his guest into the house, and set meat and drink before him; and Ulysses said, "May Jove and all the other gods requite you for the kind speeches and hospitable usage which you have shown me!"

Eumæus made answer, "My poor guest, if one in much worse plight than yourself had arrived here, it were a shame to such scanty means as I have, if I had let him depart without entertaining him to the best of my ability. Poor men, and such as have no houses of their own, are by Jove himself recommended to our care. But the cheer which we that are servants to other men have to bestow, is but sorry at most; yet freely and lovingly I give it you. Indeed there once ruled here a man, whose return the gods have set their faces against, who, if he had been suffered to reign in peace and grow old among us, would have been kind to me and mine. But he is gone; and for his sake would to God that the whole posterity of Helen might perish with her, since in her quarrel so many worthies have perished. But such as your fare is, eat it, and be welcome; such lean beasts as are food for poor herdsmen. The fattest go to feed the voracious stomachs of the queen's suitors. Shame on their unworthiness, there is no day in which two or three of the noblest of the herd are not slain to support their feasts and their surfeits."

Ulysses gave good ear to his words, and as he ate his meat, he even tore it and rent it with his teeth, for mere vexation that his fat cattle should be slain to glut the appetites of these godless suitors. And he said, "What chief or what ruler is this, that thou commendest so highly, and sayest that he perished at Troy? I am but a stranger in these parts. It may be I have heard of some such in my long travels."

Eumæus answered, "Old father, never one of all the strangers that have come to our coast with news of Ulysses being alive, could gain credit with the queen or her son yet. These travellers, to get raiment or a meal, will not stick to invent any lie. Truth is not the commodity they deal in. Never did the queen get anything of them but lies. She receives all that come graciously, hears their stories, inquires all she can, but all ends in tears and dissatisfaction. But in God's name, old father, if you have got a tale, make the most on't, it may gain you a cloak or a coat from somebody to keep you warm; but for him who is the subject of it, dogs and vultures long since have torn him limb from limb, or some great fish at sea has devoured him, or he lieth with no better monument upon his bones than the sea-sand. But for me, past all the race of men, were tears created; for I never shall find so kind a royal master more; not if my father or my mother could come again and visit me from the tomb, would my eyes be so blessed, as they should be with the sight of him again, coming as from the dead. In his last rest my soul shall love him. He is not here, nor do I name him as a flatterer, but because I am thankful for his love and care which he had to me as a poor man; and if I knew surely that he were past all shores that the sun shines upon, I would invoke him as a deified thing."

For this saying of Eumæus the waters stood in Ulysses' eyes, and he said, "My friend, to say and to affirm positively that he cannot be alive, is to give too much license to incredulity. For, not to speak at random, but with as much solemnity as an oath comes to, I say to you that Ulysses shall return, and whenever that day shall be, then shall you give to me a cloak and a coat; but till then, I will not receive so much as a thread of a garment, but rather go naked; for no less than the gates of hell do I hate that man, whom poverty can force to tell an untruth. Be Jove then witness to my words, that this very year, nay ere this month be fully ended, your eyes shall behold Ulysses, dealing vengeance in his own palace upon the wrongers of his wife and his son."

To give the better credence to his words, he amused Eumæus with a forged story of his life, feigning of himself that he was a Cretan born, and one that went with Idomeneus to the wars of Troy. Also he said that he knew Ulysses, and related various passages which he alleged to have happened betwixt Ulysses and himself; which were either true in the main, as having really happened between Ulysses and some other person, or were so like to truth, as corresponding with the known character and actions of Ulysses, that Eumæus' incredulity was not a little shaken. Among other things he asserted that he had lately been entertained in the court of Thesprotia, where the king's son of the country, had told him that Ulysses had been there but just before him, and was gone upon a voyage to the oracle of Jove in Dodona, whence he should shortly return, and a ship would be ready by the bounty of the Thesprotians to convoy him straight to Ithaca. "And in token that what I tell you is true," said Ulysses, "if your king come not within the period which I have named, you shall have leave to give your servants commandment to take my old carcase, and throw it headlong from some steep rock into the sea; that poor men, taking example by me, may fear to lie." But Eumæus made answer that that should be small satisfaction or pleasure to him.

So while they sat discoursing in this manner, supper was served in, and the servants of the herdsman, who had been out all day in the fields, came in to supper, and took their seats at the fire, for the night was bitter and frosty. After supper, Ulysses, who had well eaten and drunken, and was refreshed with the herdsman's good cheer, was resolved to try whether his host's hospitality would extend to the lending him a good warm mantle or rug to cover him in the night season; and framing an artful tale for the purpose, in a merry mood, filling a cup of Greek wine, he thus began:

"I will you a story of your king Ulysses and myself. If there is ever a time when a man may have leave to tell his own stories, it is when he has drunken a little too much. Strong liquor driveth the fool, and moves even the heart of the wise, moves and impels him to sing and to dance, and break forth in pleasant laughters, and perchance to prefer a speech too which were better kept in. When the heart is open, the tongue will be stirring. But you shall hear. We led our powers to ambush once under the walls of Troy."

The herdsmen crowded about him eager to hear anything which related to their King Ulysses and the wars of Troy, and thus he went on:

"I remember, Ulysses and Menelaus had the direction of that enterprise, and they were pleased to join me with them in the command. I was at that time in some repute among men, though fortune has played me a trick since, as you may perceive. But I was somebody in those times, and could do something. Be that as it may, a bitter freezing night it was, such a night as this, the air cut like steel, and the sleet gathered on our shields like crystal. There were some twenty of us that lay close crouched down among the reeds and bulrushes that grew in the moat that goes round the city. The rest of us made tolerable shift, for every man had been careful to bring with him a good cloak or mantle to wrap over his armour and keep himself warm; but I, as it chanced, had left my cloak behind me, as not expecting that the night would prove so cool; or rather I believe because I had at that time a brave suit of new armour on, which, being a soldier, and having some of the soldier's vice about me, *vanity*, I was not willing should be hidden under a cloak; but I paid for my indiscretion with my sufferings, for with the inclement night, and the wet of the ditch in which we lay, I was well-nigh frozen to death; and when I could endure no longer, I jogged Ulysses who was next to me, and had a nimble ear, and made known my case to him, assuring him that I must inevitably perish. He answered in a low whisper, "Hush, least any Greek should hear you, and take notice of your softness." Not a word more he said, but showed as if he had no pity for the plight I was in. But he was as considerate as he was brave, and even then, as he lay with his head reposing upon his hand, he was meditating how to relieve me, without exposing my weakness to the soldiers. At last raising up his head, he made as if he had been asleep, and said, 'Friends, I have been warned in a dream to send to the fleet to King Agamemnon for a supply, to recruit our numbers, for we are not sufficient for this enterprise;' and they believing him, one Thoas was dispatched on that errand, who departing, for more speed, as Ulysses had foreseen, left his upper garment behind him, a good warm mantle, to which I succeeded, and by the help of it got through the night with credit. This shift Ulysses made for one in need, and would to heaven that I had now that strength in my limbs, which made me in those days to be accounted fit to be a leader under Ulysses! I should not then want the loan of a cloak or mantle, to wrap about me and shield my old limbs from the night-air."

The tale pleased the herdsmen; and Eumæus, who more than all the rest was gratified to hear tales of Ulysses, true or false, said, that for his story he deserved a mantle, and a night's lodging, which he should have; and he spread for him a bed of goat and sheep skins by the fire; and the seeming beggar, who was indeed the true Ulysses, lay down and slept under that poor roof, in that abject disguise to which the will of Minerva had subjected him.

When morning was come, Ulysses made offer to depart, as if he were not willing to burthen his host's hospitality any longer, but said, that he would go and try the humanity of the town's folk, if any there would bestow upon him a bit of bread or a cup of drink. Perhaps the queen's suitors (he said) out of their full feasts would bestow a scrap on him; for he could wait at table, if need were, and play the nimble serving man; he could fetch wood (he said) or build a fire, prepare roast meat or boiled, mix the wine with water, or do any of those offices which recommended poor men like him to services in great men's houses.

"Alas! poor guest," said Eumæus, "you know not what you speak. What should so poor and old a man as you do at the suitors' tables? Their light minds are not given to such grave servitors. They must have youths richly tricked out in flowing vests, with curled hair, like so many of Jove's cup-bearers, to fill out the wine to them as they sit at table, and to shift their trenchers. Their gorged insolence would but despise and make a mock at thy age. Stay here. Perhaps the queen, or Telemachus, hearing of thy arrival, may send to thee of their bounty."

As he spake these words, the steps of one crossing the front court were heard, and a noise of the dogs fawning and leaping about as for joy; by which token Eumæus guessed that it was the prince, who hearing of a traveller being arrived at Eumæus's cottage that brought tidings of his father, was come to search the truth; and Eumæus said, "It is the tread of Telemachus, the son of king Ulysses." Before he could well speak the words, the prince was at the door, whom Ulysses rising to receive, Telemachus would not suffer that so aged a man, as he appeared, should rise to do respect to him, but he courteously and reverently took him by the hand, and inclined his head to him, as if he had surely known that it was his father indeed; but Ulysses covered his eyes with his hands, that he might not show the waters which stood in them. And Telemachus said, "Is this the man who can tell us tidings of the king my father."

"He brags himself to be a Cretan born," said Eumæus, "and that he has been a soldier and a traveller, but whether he speak the truth or not, he alone can tell. But whatsoever he has been, what he is now is apparent. Such as he appears, I give him to you; do what you will with him; his boast at present is that he is at the very best a supplicant."

"Be he what he may," said Telemachus, "I accept him at your hands. But where I should bestow him I know not, seeing that in the palace his age would not exempt him from the scorn and contempt which my mother's suitors in their light minds would be sure to fling upon him. A mercy if he escaped without blows; for they are a company of evil men, whose profession is wrongs and violence."

Ulysses answered, "Since it is free for any man to speak in presence of your greatness, I must say that my heart puts on a wolfish inclination to tear and to devour, hearing your speech, that these suitors should with such injustice rage, where you should have the rule solely. What should the cause be? do you wilfully give way to their ill manners? or has your government been such as has procured ill-will towards you from your people? or do you mistrust your kinsfolk and friends in such sort, as without trial to decline their aid? a man's kindred are they that he might trust to when extremities ran high."

Telemachus replied, "The kindred of Ulysses are few. I have no brothers to assist me in the strife. But the suitors are powerful in kindred and friends. The house of old Arcesius has had this fate from the heavens, that from old it still has been supplied with single heirs. To Arcesius Laertes only was born, from Laertes descended only Ulysses, from Ulysses I alone have sprung, whom he left so young, that from me never comfort arose to him. But the end of all rests in the hands of the gods."

Then Eumæus departing to see to some necessary business of his herds, Minerva took a woman's shape, and stood in the entry of the door, and was seen to Ulysses, but by his son she was not seen, for the presences of the gods are invisible save to those to whom they will to reveal themselves. Nevertheless the dogs which were about the door saw the goddess, and durst not bark, but went crouching and licking of the dust for fear. And giving signs to Ulysses that the time was now come in which he should make himself known to his son, by her great power she changed back his shape into the same which it was before she transformed him; and Telemachus, who saw the change, but nothing of the manner by which it was effected, only he saw the appearance of a king in the vigour of his age where but just now he had seen a worn and decrepit beggar, was struck with fear, and said, "Some god has done this house this honour;" and he turned away his eyes, and would have worshipped. But his father permitted not, but said, "Look better at me; I am no deity; why put you upon me the reputation of godhead? I am no more but thy father; I am even he; I am that Ulysses, by reason of whose absence thy youth has been exposed to such wrongs from injurious men." Then kissed he his son, nor could any longer refrain those tears which he had held under such mighty restraint before, though they would ever be forcing themselves out in spite of him; but now, as if their sluices had burst, they came out like rivers, pouring upon the warm cheeks of his son. Nor yet by all these violent arguments could Telemachus be persuaded to believe that it was his father, but he said, some deity had taken that shape to mock him; for he affirmed, that it was not in the power of any man, who is sustained by mortal food, to change his shape so in a moment from age to youth; for "but now," said he, "you were all wrinkles, and were old, and now you look as the gods are pictured."

His father replied, "Admire, but fear not, and know me to be at all parts substantially thy father, who in the inner powers of his mind, and the unseen workings of a father's love to thee, answers to his outward shape and pretence! There shall no more Ulysseses come here. I am he that after twenty years' absence, and suffering a world of ill, have recovered at last the sight of my country earth. It was the will of Minerva that I should be changed as you saw me. She put me thus together; she puts together or takes to pieces whom she pleases. It is in the law of her free power to do it; sometimes to show her favourites under a cloud, and poor, and again to restore to them her ornaments. The gods raise and throw down men with ease."

Then Telemachus could hold out no longer, but he gave way now to a full belief and persuasion, of that which for joy at first he could not credit, that it was indeed his true and very father that stood before him; and they embraced, and mingled their tears.

Then said Ulysses, "Tell me who these suitors are, what are their numbers, and how stands the queen thy mother affected to them?"

"She bears them still in expectation," said Telemachus, "which she never means to fulfil, that she will accept the hand of some one of them in second nuptials. For she fears to displease them by an absolute refusal. So from day to day she lingers them on with hope, which they are content to bear the deferring of, while they have entertainment at free cost in our palace."

Then said Ulysses, "Reckon up their numbers that we may know their strength and ours, if we having none but ourselves may hope to prevail against them."

"O father," he replied, "I have oft-times heard of your fame for wisdom, and of the great strength of your arm, but the venturous mind which your speeches now indicate moves me even to amazement; for in no wise can it consist with wisdom or a sound mind, that two should try their strength against a host. Nor five, nor ten, nor twice ten strong are these suitors, but many more by much. From Dulichium came there fifty and two, they and their servants; twice twelve crossed the seas hither from Samos; from Zacynthus twice ten; of our native Ithacans, men of chief note, are twelve who aspire to the crown of Penelope; and all these under one strong roof, a fearful odds against two! My father, there is need of caution, lest the cup which your great mind so thirsts to taste of, vengeance, prove bitter to yourself in the drinking. And therefore it were well that we would bethink us of someone who might assist us in this undertaking."

"Thinkest thou," said his father, "if we had Minerva and the king of skies to be our friends, would their sufficiencies make strong our part; or must we look out for some further aid yet?"

"They you speak of are above the clouds," said Telemachus, "and are sound aids indeed; as powers that not only exceed human, but bear the chiefest sway among the gods themselves."

Then Ulysses gave directions to his son, to go and mingle with the suitors, and in no wise to impart his secret to any, not even to the queen his mother, but to hold himself in readiness, and to have his weapons and his good armour in preparation. And he charged him, that when he himself should come to the palace, as he meant to follow shortly after, and present himself in his beggar's likeness to the suitors, that whatever he should see which might grieve his heart, with what foul usage and contumelious language soever the suitors should receive his father, coming in that shape, though they should strike and drag him by the heels along the floors, that he should not stir nor make offer to oppose them, further than by mild words to expostulate with them; until Minerva from heaven should give the sign which should be the prelude to their destruction. And Telemachus promising to obey his instructions departed; and the shape of Ulysses fell to what it had been before, and he became to all outward appearance a beggar, in base and beggarly attire.

Chapter 9

The queen's suitors. The battle of the beggars. The armour taken down. The meeting with Penelope.

FROM the house of Eumæus the seeming beggar took his way, leaning on his staff, till he reached the palace, entering in at the hall where the suitors sat at meat. They in the pride of their feasting began to break their jests in mirthful manner, when they saw one looking so poor and so aged approach. He, who expected no better entertainment was nothing moved at their behaviour, but, as became the character which he had assumed, in a suppliant posture crept by turns to every suitor, and held out his hands for some charity, with such a natural and beggar-resembling grace, that he might seem to have practised begging all his life; yet there was a sort of dignity in his most abject stoopings, that whoever had seen him, would have said, If it had pleased heaven that this poor man had been born a king, he would gracefully have filled a throne. And some pitied him, and some gave him alms, as their present humours inclined them; but the greater part reviled him, and bid him begone, as one that spoiled their feast; for the presence of misery has this power with it, that while it stays, it can dash and overturn the mirth even of those who feel no pity or wish to relieve it; nature bearing this witness of herself in the hearts of the most obdurate.

Now Telemachus sat at meat with the suitors, and knew that it was the king his father, who in that shape begged an alms; and when his father came and presented himself before him in turn, as he had done to the suitors, one by one, he gave him of his own meat which he had in his dish, and of his own cup to drink. And the suitors were past measure offended to see a pitiful beggar, as they esteemed him, to be so choicely regarded by the prince.

Then Antinous, who was a great lord, and of chief note among the suitors, said, "Prince Telemachus does ill to encourage these wandering beggars, who go from place to place, affirming that they have been some considerable persons in their time, filling the ears of such as hearken to them with lies, and pressing with their bold feet into kings' palaces. This is some saucy vagabond, some travelling Egyptian."

"I see," said Ulysses, "that a poor man should get but little at your board; scarce should he get salt from your hands, if he brought his own meat."

Lord Antinous, indignant to be answered with such sharpness by a supposed beggar, snatched up a stool, with which he smote Ulysses where the neck and shoulders join. This usage moved not Ulysses; but in his great heart he meditated deep evils to come upon them all, which for a time must be kept close, and he went and sat himself down in the doorway to eat of that which was given him, and he said, "For life or possessions a man will fight, but for his belly this man smites. If a poor man has any god to take his part, my lord Antinous shall not live to be the queen's husband."

Then Antinous raged highly, and threatened to drag him by the heels, and to rend his rags about his ears, if he spoke another word.

But the other suitors did in no wise approve of the harsh language, nor of the blow which Antinous had dealt; and some of them said, "Who knows but one of the deities goes about, hid under that poor disguise? for in the likeness of poor pilgrims the gods have many times descended to try the dispositions of men, whether they be humane or impious." While these things passed, Telemachus sat and observed all, but held his peace, remembering the instructions of his father. But secretly he waited for the sign which Minerva was to send from heaven.

That day there followed Ulysses to the court one of the common sort of beggars, Irus by name, one that had received alms before-time of the suitors, and was their ordinary sport, when they were inclined (as that day) to give way to mirth, to see him eat and drink; for he had the appetite of six men, and was of huge stature and proportions of body, yet had in him no spirit nor courage of a man. This man thinking to curry favour with the suitors, and recommend himself especially to such a great lord as Antinous was, began to revile and scorn Ulysses, putting foul language upon him, and fairly challenging him to fight with the fist. But Ulysses deeming his railings to be nothing more than jealousy and that envious disposition which beggars commonly manifest to brothers in their trade, mildly besought him not to trouble him, but to enjoy that portion which the liberality of their entertainers gave him, as he did, quietly; seeing that, of their bounty, there was sufficient for all.

But Irus thinking that this forbearance in Ulysses was nothing more than a sign of fear, so much the more highly stormed, and bellowed, and provoked him to fight; and by this time the quarrel had attracted the notice of the suitors, who with loud laughters and shouting egged on the dispute; and lord Antinous swore by all the gods it should be a battle, and that in that hall the strife should be determined. To this the rest of the suitors with violent clamours acceded, and a circle was made for the combatants, and a fat goat was proposed as the victor's prize, as at the Olympic or the Pythian games. Then Ulysses seeing no remedy, or being not unwilling that the suitors should behold some proof of that strength which ere long in their own persons they were to taste of, stripped himself, and prepared for the combat. But first he demanded that he should have fair play shown him, that none in that assembly should aid his opponent, or take part against him, for, being an old man, they might easily crush him with their strengths. And Telemachus passed his word that no foul play should be shown him, but that each party should be left to their own unassisted strengths, and to this he made Antinous and the rest of the suitors swear.

But when Ulysses had laid aside his garments, and was bare to the waist, all the beholders admired at the goodly sight of his large shoulders, being of such exquisite shape and whiteness; and at his great and brawny bosom, and the youthful strength which seemed to remain in a man thought so old; and they said, "What limbs and what sinews he has!" and coward fear seized on the mind of that great vast beggar, and he dropped his threats and big words, and would have fled. But lord Antinous stayed him, and threatened him that if he declined the combat, he would put him in a ship, and land him on the shores where king Echetus reigned, the roughest tyrant which at that time the world contained, and who had that antipathy to rascal beggars, such as he, that when any landed on his coast, he would crop their ears and noses, and give them to the dogs to tear. So Irus, in whom fear of king Echetus prevailed above the fear of Ulysses, addressed himself to fight. But Ulysses, provoked to be engaged in so odious a strife with a fellow of his base conditions, and loathing longer to be made a spectacle to entertain the eyes of his foes, with one blow which he struck him beneath the ear, so shattered the teeth and jawbone of this soon baffled coward, that he laid him sprawling in the dust, with small stomach or ability to renew the contest. Then raising him on his feet, he led him bleeding and sputtering to the door, and put his staff into his hand, and bid him go use his command upon dogs and swine, but not presume himself to be lord of the guests another time, nor of the beggary!

The suitors applauded in their vain minds the issue of the contest, and rioted in mirth at the expense of poor Irus, who they vowed should be forthwith embarked, and sent to king Echetus; and they bestowed thanks on Ulysses for ridding the court of that unsavory morsel, as they called him; but in their inward souls they would not have cared if Irus had been victor, and Ulysses had taken the foil, but it was mirth to them to see the beggars fight. In such pastimes and light entertainments the day wore away.

When evening was come the suitors betook themselves to music and dancing. And Ulysses leaned his back against a pillar from which certain lamps hung which gave light to the dancers, and he made show of watching the dancers, but very different thoughts were in his head. And as he stood near the lamps, the light fell upon his head, which was thin of hair and bald, as an old man's. And Eurymachus, a suitor, taking occasion from some words which were spoken before, scoffed and said, "Now I know for a certainty that some god lurks under the poor and beggarly appearance of this man; for as he stands by the lamps, his sleek head throws beams around it, like as it were a glory." And another said, "He passes his time too not much unlike the gods, lazily living exempt from labour, taking offerings of men." "I warrant," said Eurymachus again, "he could not raise a fence or dig a ditch for his livelihood, if a man would hire him to work in a garden."

"I wish," said Ulysses, "that you who speak this, and myself, were to be tried at any task-work; that I had a good crooked scythe put in my hand, that was sharp and strong, and you such another, where the grass grew longest, to be up by day-break, mowing the meadows till the sun went down, not tasting of food till we had finished; or that we were set to plough four acres in one day of good glebe land, to see whose furrows were evenest and cleanest; or that we might have one wrestling bout together; or that in our right hands a good steel-headed lance were placed, to try whose blows fell heaviest and thickest upon the adversary's head-piece. I would cause you such work, as you should have small reason to reproach me with being slack at work. But you would do well to spare me this reproach, and to save your strength, till the owner of this house shall return, till the day when Ulysses shall return, when returning he shall enter upon his birthright."

This was a galling speech to those suitors, to whom Ulysses' return was indeed the thing which they most dreaded. And a sudden fear fell upon their souls, as if they were sensible of the real presence of that man who did indeed stand amongst them, but not in that form as they might know him; and Eurymachus, incensed, snatched a massy cup which stood on a table near, and hurled it at the head of the supposed beggar, and but narrowly missed the hitting of him; and all the suitors rose, as at once, to thrust him out of the hall, which they said his beggarly presence and his rude speeches had profaned. But Telemachus cried to hem to forbear, and not to presume to lay hands upon a wretched man to whom he had promised protection. He asked if they were mad, to mix such abhorred uproar with his feasts. He bade them take their food and their wine, to sit up or to go to bed at their free pleasures, so long as he should give licence to that freedom; but why should they abuse his banquet, or let the words which a poor beggar spake have power to move their spleens so fiercely?

They bit their lips and frowned for anger, to be checked so by a youth; nevertheless for that time they had the grace to abstain, either for shame, or that Minerva had infused into them a terror of Ulysses' son.

So that day's feast was concluded without bloodshed, and the suitors, tired with their sports, departed severally each man to his apartment. Only Ulysses and Telemachus remained. And now Telemachus, by his father's direction went and brought down into the hall armour and lances from the armoury; for Ulysses said, "On the morrow we shall have need of them." And moreover, he said, "If any one shall ask why you have taken them down, say, it is to clean them and scour them from the rust which they have gathered since the owner of this house went for Troy." And as Telemachus stood by the armour, the lights were all gone out, and it was pitch-dark, and the armour gave out glistening beams as of fire, and he said to his father, "The pillars of the house are on fire." And his father said, "It is the gods who sit above the stars, and have power to make the night as light as the day." And he took it for a good omen. And Telemachus fell to cleaning and sharpening of the lances.

Now Ulysses had not seen his wife Penelope in all the time since his return; for the queen did not care to mingle with the suitors at their banquets, but, as became one that had been Ulysses' wife, kept much in private, spinning and doing her excellent housewiveries among her maids in the remote apartments of the palace. Only upon solemn days she would come down and show herself to the suitors. And Ulysses was filled with a longing desire to see his wife again, whom for twenty years he had not beheld, and he softly stole through the known passages of his beautiful house, till he came where the maids were lighting the queen through a stately gallery that led to the chamber where she slept. And when the maids saw Ulysses, they said, "It is the beggar who came to the court to-day, about whom all that uproar was stirred up in the hall: what does he here?" But Penelope gave commandment that he should be brought before her, for she said, "It may be that he has travelled, and has heard something concerning Ulysses."

Then was Ulysses right glad to hear himself named by his queen, to find himself in nowise forgotten, nor her great love towards him decayed in all that time that he had been away. And he stood before his queen, and she knew him not to be Ulysses, but supposed that he had been some poor traveller. And she asked him of what country he was.

He told her (as he had before told to Eumæus) that he was a Cretan born, and however poor and cast down he now seemed, no less a man than brother to Idomeneus, who was grandson to King Minos, and though he now wanted bread, he had once had it in his power to feast Ulysses. Then he feigned how Ulysses, sailing for Troy, was forced by stress of weather to put his fleet in at a port of Crete, where for twelve days he was his guest, and entertained by him with all befitting guest-rites. And he described the very garments which Ulysses had on, by which Penelope knew that he had seen her lord.

In this manner Ulysses told his wife many tales of himself, at most but painting, but painting so near to the life, that the feeling of that which she took in at her ears became so strong, that the kindly tears ran down her fair cheeks, while she thought upon her lord, dead she thought him, and heavily mourned the loss of him whom she missed, whom she could not find, though in very deed he stood so near her.

Ulysses was moved to see her weep, but he kept his own eyes as dry as iron or horn in their lids, putting a bridle upon his strong passion, that it should not issue to sight.

Then told he how he had lately been at the court of Thesprotia, and what he had learned concerning Ulysses there, in order as he had delivered to Eumæus. And Penelope was won to believe that there might be a possibility of Ulysses being alive, and she said, "I dreamed a dream this morning. Methought I had twenty household fowl which did eat wheat steeped in water from my hand, and there came suddenly from the clouds a crook-beaked hawk who soused on them and killed them all, trussing their necks, then took his flight back up to the clouds. And in my dream methought that I wept and made great moan for my fowls, and for the destruction which the hawk had made; and my maids came about me to comfort me. And in the height of my griefs the hawk came back, and lighting upon the beam of my chamber, he said to me in a man's voice, which sounded strangely even in my dream, to hear a hawk to speak: 'Be of good cheer,' he said, 'O daughter of Icarius; for this is no dream which thou hast seen, but that which shall happen to thee indeed. Those household fowl which thou lamentest so without reason, are the suitors who devour thy substance, even as thou sawest the fowl eat from thy hand, and the hawk is thy husband, who is coming to give death to the suitors.' And I awoke, and went to see to my fowls if they were alive, whom I found eating wheat from their troughs, all well and safe as before my dream."

Then said Ulysses, "This dream can endure no other interpretation than that which the hawk gave to it, who is your lord, and who is coming quickly to effect all that his words told you."

"Your words," she said, "my old guest, are so sweet, that would you sit and please me with your speech, my ears would never let my eyes close their spheres for very joy of your discourse; but none that is merely mortal can live without the death of sleep; so the gods who are without death themselves have ordained it, to keep the memory of our mortality in our minds, while we experience that as much as we live we die every day; in which consideration I will ascend my bed, which I have nightly watered with my tears since he that was the joy of it departed for that bad city;" she so speaking, because she could not bring her lips to name the name of Troy so much hated. So for that night they parted, Penelope to her bed, and Ulysses to his son, and to the armour and the lances in the hall, where they sat up all night cleaning and watching by the armour.

Chapter 10

The madness from above. The bow of Ulysses. The slaughter. The conclusion.

WHEN daylight appeared, a tumultuous concourse of suitors again filled the hall; and some wondered, and some inquired what meant that glittering store of armour and lances which lay on heaps by the entry of the door; and to all that asked Telemachus made reply, that he had caused them to be taken down to cleanse them of the rust and of the stain which they had contracted by lying so long unused, even ever since his father went for Troy; and with that answer their minds were easily satisfied. So to their feasting and vain rioting again they fell. Ulysses by Telemachus' order had a seat and a mess assigned him in the door-way, and he had his eye ever on the lances. And it moved gall in some of the great ones there present to have their feast still dulled with the society of that wretched beggar, as they deemed him, and they reviled and spurned at him with their feet. Only there was one Philætius, who had something a better nature than the rest, that spake kindly to him, and had his age in respect. He coming up to Ulysses, took him by the hand with a kind of fear, as if touched exceedingly with imagination of his great worth, and said thus to him, "Hail! father stranger! my brows have sweat to see the injuries which you have received, and my eyes have broke forth in tears, when I have only thought that such being oftentimes the lot of worthiest men, to this plight Ulysses may be reduced, and that he now may wander from place to place as you do; for such who are compelled by need to range here and there, and have no firm home to fix their feet upon, God keeps them in this earth, as under water; so are they kept down and depressed. And a dark thread is sometimes spun in the fates of kings."

At this bare likening of the beggar to Ulysses, Minerva from heaven made the suitors for foolish joy to go mad, and roused them to such a laughter as would never stop, they laughed without power of ceasing, their eyes stood full of tears for violent joys; but fears and horrible misgivings succeeded; and one among them stood up and prophesied: "Ah, wretches!" he said, "what madness from heaven has seized you, that you can laugh? see you not that your meat drops blood? a night, like the night of death, wraps you about, you shriek without knowing it; your eyes thrust forth tears; the fixed walls, and the beam that bears the whole house up, fall blood; ghosts choke up the entry; full is the hall with apparitions of murdered men; under your feet is hell; the sun falls from heaven, and it is midnight at noon." But like men whom the gods had infatuated to their destruction, they mocked at his fears, and Eurymachus said, "This man is surely mad, conduct him forth into the market-place, set him in the light, for he dreams that 'tis night within the house."

But Theoclymenus (for that was the prophet's name), whom Minerva had graced with a prophetic spirit, that he, foreseeing might avoid the destruction which awaited them, answered and said, "Eurymachus, I will not require a guide of thee, for I have eyes and ears, the use of both my feet, and a sane mind within me, and with these I will go forth of the doors, because I know the imminent evils which await all you that stay, by reason of this poor guest who is a favourite with all the gods."

So saying he turned his back upon those inhospitable men, and went away home, and never returned to the palace.

These words which he spoke were not unheard by Telemachus, who kept still his eye upon his father, expecting fervently when he would give the sign, which was to precede the slaughter of the suitors.

They dreaming of no such thing, fell sweetly to their dinner, as joying in the great store of banquet which was heaped in full tables about them; but there reigned not a bitterer banquet planet in all heaven, than that which hung over them this day by secret destination of Minerva.

There was a bow which Ulysses left when he went for Troy. It had lain by since that time, out of use and unstrung, for no man had strength to draw the bow, save Ulysses. So it had remained, as a monument of the great strength of its master. This bow, with the quiver of arrows belonging thereto, Telemachus had brought down from the armoury on the last night along with the lances; and now Minerva, intending to do Ulysses an honour, put it into the mind of Telemachus to propose to the suitors to try who was strongest to draw that bow; and he promised that to the man who should be able to draw that bow, his mother should be given in marriage; Ulysses' wife the prize to him who should bend the bow of Ulysses.

There was great strife and emulation stirred up among the suitors at those words of the Prince Telemachus. And to grace her son's words, and to confirm the promise which he had made, Penelope came and showed herself that day to the suitors; and Minerva made her that she appeared never so comely in their sight as that day, and they were inflamed with the beholding of so much beauty, proposed as the price of so great manhood; and they cried out, that if all those heroes who sailed to Colchos for the rich purchase of the golden-fleeced ram, had seen earth's richer prize, Penelope, they would not have made their voyage, but would have vowed their valours and their lives to her, for she was at all parts faultless.

And she said, "The gods have taken my beauty from me, since my lord went for Troy." But Telemachus willed his mother to depart and not be present at that contest, for he said, "It maybe, some rougher strife shall chance of this, than may be expedient for a woman to witness." And she retired, she and her maids, and left the hall.

Then the bow was brought into the midst, and a mark was set up by prince Telemachus; and Lord Antinous as the chief among the suitors had the first offer, and he took the bow, and fitting an arrow to the string, he strove to bend it; but not with all his might and main could he once draw together the ends of that tough bow; and when he found how vain a thing it was to endeavour to draw Ulysses' bow, he desisted, blushing for shame and for mere anger. Then Eurymachus adventured, but with no better success; but as it had torn the hands of Antinous, so did the bow tear and strain his hands, and marred his delicate fingers, yet could he not once stir the strings. Then called he to the attendants to bring fat and unctuous matter, which melting at the fire, he dipped the bow therein, thinking to supple it and make it more pliable; but not with all the helps of art could he succeed in making it to move. After him Liodes, and Amphinomus, and Polybus, and Eurynomus, and Polyctorides, assayed their strength, but not any one of them, or of the rest of those aspiring suitors, had any better luck; yet not the meanest of them there but thought himself well worthy of Ulysses' wife, though to shoot with Ulysses' bow the completest champion among them was by proof found too feeble.

Then Ulysses prayed them that he might have leave to try; and immediately a clamour was raised among the suitors because of his petition, and they scorned and swelled with rage at his presumption, and that a beggar should seek to contend in a game of such noble mastery. But Telemachus ordered that the bow should be given him, and that he should have leave to try, since they had failed; "for," he said, "the bow is mine, to give or to withhold." And none durst gainsay the prince.

Then Ulysses gave a sign to his son, and he commanded the doors of the hall to be made fast, and all wondered at his words, but none could divine the cause. And Ulysses took the bow into his hands, and before he essayed to bend it, he surveyed it at all parts to see whether, by long lying by, it had contracted any stiffness which hindered the drawing; and as he was busied in the curious surveying of his bow, some of the suitors mocked him and said, "Past doubt this man is a right cunning archer, and knows his craft well. See how he turns it over and over, and looks into it as if he could see through the wood." And others said, "We wish some one would tell out gold into our laps but for so long a time as he shall be in drawing of that string." But when he had spent some little time in making proof of the bow, and had found it to be in good plight, like as a harper in tuning of his harp draws out a string, with such ease or much more did Ulysses draw to the head the string of his own tough bow, and in letting of it go, it twanged with such a shrill noise as a swallow makes when it sings through the air; which so much amazed the suitors that their colours came and went, and the skies gave out a noise of thunder, which at heart cheered Ulysses, for he knew that now his long labours by the disposal of the fates drew to an end. Then fitted he an arrow to the bow, and drawing it to the head, he sent it right to the mark which the prince had set up. Which done, he said to Telemachus, "You have got no disgrace yet by your guest, for I have struck the mark I shot at, and gave myself no such trouble in teasing the bow with fat and fire as these men did, but have made proof that my strength is not impaired, nor my age so weak and contemptible as these were pleased to think it. But come, the day going down calls us to supper, after which succeed poem and harp, and all delights which use to crown princely banquettings."

So saying, he beckoned to his son, who straight girt his sword to his side, and took one of the lances (of which there lay great store from the armoury) in his hand, and armed at all points, advanced towards his father.

The upper rags which Ulysses wore fell from his shoulder, and his own kingly likeness returned, when he rushed to the great hall door with bow and quiver full of shafts, which down at his feet he poured, and in bitter words presignified his deadly intent to the suitors. "Thus far," he said, "this contest has been decided harmless; now for us there rests another mark, harder to hit, but which my hands shall essay notwithstanding, if Phoebus, god of archers, be pleased to give me mastery." With that he let fly a deadly arrow at Antinous, which pierced him in the throat as he was in the act of lifting a cup of wine to his mouth. Amazement seized the suitors, as their great champion fell dead, and they raged highly against Ulysses, and said that it should prove the dearest shaft which he ever let fly, for he had slain a man, whose like breathed not in any part of the kingdom: and they flew to their arms, and would have seized the lances, but Minerva struck them with dimness of sight, that they went erring up and down the hall, not knowing where to find them. Yet so infatuated were they by the displeasure of heaven, that they did not see the imminent peril which impended over them, but every man believed that this accident had happened beside the intention of the doer. Fools! to think by shutting their eyes to evade destiny, or that any other cup remained for them, but that which their great Antinous had tasted!

Then Ulysses revealed himself to all in that presence, and that he was the man whom they held to be dead at Troy, whose palace they had usurped, whose wife in his lifetime they had sought in impious marriage, and that for this reason destruction was come upon them. And he dealt his deadly arrows among them, and there was no avoiding him, nor escaping from his horrid person, and Telemachus by his side plied them thick with those murderous lances from which there was no retreat, till fear itself made them valiant, and danger gave them eyes to understand the peril. Then they which had swords drew them, and some with shields, that could find them, and some with tables and benches snatched up in haste, rose in a mass to overwhelm and crush those two; yet they singly bestirred themselves like men, and defended themselves against that great host; and through tables, shields and all, right through, the arrows of Ulysses clove, and the irresistible lances of Telemachus; and many lay dead, and all had wounds. And Minerva in the likeness of a bird sate upon the beam which went across the hall, clapping her wings with a fearful noise; and sometimes the great bird would fly among them, cuffing at the swords and at the lances, and up and down the hall would go, beating her wings, and troubling everything, that it was frightful to behold, and it frayed the blood from the cheeks of those heaven-hated suitors. But to Ulysses and his son she appeared in her own divine similitude, with her snake-fringed shield, a goddess armed, fighting their battles. Nor did that dreadful pair desist, till they had laid all their foes at their feet. At their feet they lay in shoals; like fishes, when the fishermen break up their nets, so they lay gasping and sprawling at the feet of Ulysses and his son. And Ulysses remembered the prediction of Tiresias, which said that he was to perish by his own guests, unless he slew those who knew him not.

Then certain of the queen's household went up and told Penelope what had happened, and how her lord Ulysses had come home, and had slain the suitors. But she gave no heed to their words, but thought that some frenzy possessed them, or that they mocked her; for it s the property of such extremes of sorrow as she had felt, not to believe when any great joy cometh. And she rated and chid them exceedingly for troubling her. But they the more persisted in their asseverations of the truth of what they had affirmed; and some of them had seen the slaughtered bodies of the suitors dragged forth of the hall. And they said, "That poor guest whom you talked with last night was Ulysses." Then she was yet more fully persuaded that they mocked her, and she wept.

But they said, "This thing is true which we have told. We sat within, in an inner room in the palace, and the doors of the hall were shut on us, but we heard the cries and the groans of the men that were killed, but saw nothing till at length your son called to us to come in, and entering we saw Ulysses standing in the midst of the slaughtered." But she persisting in her unbelief, said, that it was some god which had deceived them to think it was the person of Ulysses.

By this time Telemachus and his father had cleansed their hands from the slaughter, and were come to where the queen was talking with those of her household; and when she saw Ulysses, she stood motionless, and had no power to speak, sudden surprise and joy and fear and many passions so strove within her. Sometimes she was clear that it was her husband that she saw, and sometimes the alteration which twenty years had made in his person (yet that was not much) perplexed her that she knew not what to think, and for joy she could not believe; and yet for joy she would not but believe; and above all, that sudden change from a beggar to a king troubled her, and wrought uneasy scruples in her mind. But Telemachus seeing her strangeness, blamed her, and called her an ungentle and tyrannous mother; and said that she showed a too great curiousness of modesty, to abstain from embracing his father, and to have doubts of his person, when to all present it was evident that he was the very real and true Ulysses.

Then she mistrusted no longer, but ran and fell upon Ulysses' neck, and said, "Let not my husband be angry, that I held off so long with strange delays; it is the gods, who severing us for so long time, have caused this unseemly distance in me. If Menelaus' wife had used half my caution, she would never have taken so freely to a stranger; and she might have spared us all these plagues which have come upon us through her."

These words with which Penelope excused herself, wrought more affection in Ulysses than if upon a first sight she had given up herself implicitly to his embraces; and he wept for joy to possess a wife so discreet, so answering to his own staid mind, that had a depth of wit proportioned to his own, and one that held chaste virtue at so high a price. And he thought the possession of such a one cheaply purchased with the loss of all Circe's delights, and Calypso's immortality of joys; and his long labours and his severe sufferings past seemed as nothing, now they were crowned with the enjoyment of his virtuous and true wife, Penelope. And as sad men at sea whose ship has gone to pieces nigh shore, swimming for their lives, all drenched in foam and brine, crawl up to some poor patch of land, which they take possession of with as great joy as if they had the world given them in fee, with such delight did this chaste wife cling to her lord restored.

So from that time the land had rest from the suitors. And the happy Ithacans with songs and solemn sacrifices of praise to the gods celebrated the return of Ulysses; for he that had been so long absent was returned to wreak the evil upon the heads of the doers; in the place where they had done the evil, there wreaked he his vengeance upon them.

Index of Proper Names

A

Acheron
>Ach'erön

Achilles
>Achil'lës

Ææa
>Æǽ'á

Ægisthus
>Ægis'thus

Æthiopians
>Æthiö'pians

Agamemnon
>Ägämem'nön

Ajax
>Ä'jax

Alcinous
>Alcïn'öüs

Alcmena
>Alcmë'na

Amphinomus
>Amphin'ömus

Antiphas
>An'tïphas

Apollo
>Ápol'lo

Arcesius
>Arcë'siüs

Argo
>Argo

Ariadne
>Aríád'në

Atreus

A'trëus

B

Bear

Bear

Bootes

Bóö'tës

Boreas

Bó'réas

C

Cadmus

Cad'mus

Calliroe

Callír'óë

Calypso

Cályp'sö

Castor

Cas'tor

Charybdis

Cháryb'dis

Cicons

Cíc'ons

Circe

Cir'cë

Clytemnestra

Clýt'emnes'tra

Cocytus

Cöcÿ'tus

Colchos

Col'chós

Cratis

Cra'tis

Crete

Crete

Cyclops

Cÿclöps

Cythera

    Cýthë'ra

D

Deiphobus

    Dëíph'óbus

Delos

    Dë'los

Demodocus

    Dëmód'ócus

Diana

    Dïä'na

Dodona

    Dödö'na

Dulichium

    Dülích'íúm

E

Echetus

    Éch'étus

Ephialtes

    Éph'íal'tës

Eriphyle

    Ér'íphÿ'lë

Eumæus

    Eumæ'us

Eurus

    Eu'rus

Eurylochus

    Eurýl'óchus

Eurymachus

    Eurým'áchus

Eurynomus

    Eurýn'ómus

F

Fates

    Fates

H

Hades

    Hä'dës

Helena

    Hél'éna

Hercules

    Her'cúlës

I

Icarius

    Ïcá'ríús

Idomeneus

    Ïdóm'éneus

Ino Leucothea

    Ïnö Lëucó'théá

Iphimedeia

    Iph'ímédei'a

Irus

    Ï'rús

Ismarus

    Is'márus

Ithaca

    Ith'ácá

J

Jove

    Jöve

L

Laertes

    Läer'tës

Læstrygonians

    Læstrÿgó'níans

Lamos

    Lá'mos

Latona

    Lätö'na

Leda

    Lë'da

Liodes

Liö'dës

M

Malea

Málé'á

Menelaus

Mén'élä'ús

Mentor

Men'tor

Mercury

Mer'cúry

Minerva

Míner'va

Minos

Mi'nös

N

Naids

Nä'iads

Nausicaa

Nausíc'áá

Neoptolemus

Né'optól'émus

Neptune

Nep'tüne

Nerytus

Nër'ýtús

Notus

Nó'tus

O

Ogygia

Ögýg'ía

Olympus

Ölym'pus

Orchomen

Orchó'men

Orestes

Óres'tës

Orion

Öri'on

Ossa

Os'sa

Otus

Ö'tus

P

Panopeus

Pánó'peus

Peleus

Pë'leus

Pelion

Pë'líon

Penelope

Pënel'ópë

Phæacians

Phæä'cíans

Phædra

Phæ'dra

Philætius

Phílæ'tíús

Phoebus

Phoe'bus

Pieria

Pi'érí'á

Pirithous

Piríth'óús

Pleiads

Ple'iads

Pluto

Plu'to

Pollux

Pol'lux

Polybus

Pól'ýbús

Polyctorides

Pólyctór'ídës

Polyphemus

Pólyphë'mus

Procris

Pró'cris

Proserpine

Próser'pine

Pylus

Py'lus

Pyriphlegethon

Pýriphlég'éthön

Pytho

Pÿ'thö

S

Samos

Sá'mós

Scylla

Scýl'la

Scyros

Scÿ'rós

Sirens

Sï'rens

Sisyphus

Sïs'ýphús

Smyrna

Smyr'na

Solymi

Sól'ýmï

Sparta

Spar'ta

Styx

Styx

T

Tantalus

Tan'tálús

Telamon

Tél'ámön

Telemachus

Tëlém'áchús

Theseus

Thë'sëus

Thesprotia

Thesprötíá

Thetis

Thé'tís

Tiresias

Tíré'siäs

Tityus

Tit'ýús

Trinacria

Trïná'críá

Troy

Troy

Tyndarus

Tyn'dárús

Z

Zacynthus

Zácyn'thús

Zephyrus

Zéph'ýrús

Notes

(John Cooke, 1892)

Troy -- The capital of Troas, so called from a king of that name, on the west of Asia Minor situated on a small eminence near Mount Ida, about four miles from the sea coast. Its war was the most celebrated in ancient times. (See Introduction).

Ithaca -- One of the Ionian Islands, off the west coast of Greece, and separated from the larger island of Cephalonia by a channel three or four miles wide. It is twelve miles long by four broad. The home of Ulysses was on a precipitous cliff situated on a narrow isthmus connecting the two parts of the island. This "eagle cliff" is pronounced to be about as bleak and dreary a spot as can well be imagined for a princely residence.

Calypso -- One of the Oceanides, or sea nymphs, who dwelt in Ogygia, an island of doubtful existence, and whose position is unknown. Here Ulysses was shipwrecked, and remained for seven years. These nymphs could protect or injure sailors; hence sacrifices and prayers were offered to them.

Circe -- The daughter of Sol, the Sun, celebrated for her knowledge of magic and poisons. She murdered her husband, the Prince of Colchis, a country east of the Euxine or Black Sea, and, being banished from the kingdom, was carried to the island of Æxa, off the coast of Italy, where Ulysses, allured by her, remained a year.

Cicons -- A people of Thrace, that part of modern Turkey between the Balkan Mountains and the Archipelago, who assisted the Trojans against the Greeks.

Ismarus -- The chief town of the Cicons, situated on a mountain of the same name, celebrated for its wine.

Malea -- A cape at the end of the promontory in the Morea, lying between the gulfs of Nauplia and Laconia. The sea round it being so rough, it was much dreaded by sailors.

Cythera -- An island off the south coast of Greece near Cape Malea, now called Cerigo. It was particularly sacred to the goddess Venus, who sprung from the foam of the sea, near its coast, according to some traditions, and who was hence called Cytheræa.

lotos-tree -- [lotus] This name was given to various plants whose fruit or berry was used for food, and from which wine was also made. The *lotophagi,* or lotos-eaters, were a peaceful people, who dwelt on the coast of Libya, in the north of Africa. The fable of strangers eating the fruit of the lotos, and forgetting their native country, was a common one in ancient times. Tennyson wrote a short poem on "The Lotos-Eaters," in "A land where all things seem'd the same," and where he who received of the lotos fruit and tasted it--

"To him the gushing of the wave
Far, far away did seem to mourn and rave
On alien shores; and if his fellow spake,
His voice was thin, as voices from the grave;
And deep-asleep he seem'd, yet all awake,
And music in his heart his beating heart did make."

hatches -- The lid, cover, or frame of cross-bars laid over the hatchway or opening of a ship's deck. "Under the hatches" means to be confined below, under the deck.

Cyclops -- Creatures with round eyes. (Gr. *kyklopes* = *kyklos,* a circle, and *ops* an eye.) They had but one great round eye in the centre of the forehead, and hence their name. According to Homer they inhabited Sicily, and were a lawless race of shepherds, and cannibals, or human flesh-eaters, without any knowledge of law or order, living separately with their families in caverns among the mountains. They cared nothing for the gods, and deemed themselves their superior in strength. They were also supposed to have made the lightning and thunderbolts of Jupiter, and to have assisted Vulcan, whose workshops were volcanoes, in making armour for the gods and heroes. The ancients considered that great and massive unhewn stone walls and fortresses were their work; and hence the term "cyclopian" applied to walls and structures of which history has left us little or no account.

outlandish -- Rude, barbarous. Originally, foreign, as "*outlandish* women," Nehemiah xiii. 26. From A-S. *utlaendisc,* out, and *land.*

Greek wine -- wine was known to the Greeks from the earliest times. It was extracted from the ripe grape and from the raisin. The valleys, mountain slopes, and islands of their country were celebrated for the vine. When the wine was made it was drunk fresh, or, after cleansing by various methods and straining, it was preserved in skins. That used by Ulysses would be kept in a goat-skin, pitched over to keep the seams tight. It was given to him by the priest of Apollo at Ismarus, and was so precious that none knew of it there but himself, wife, and the keeper of it.

flagon -- A vessel with a narrow mouth used for holding liquors. It was larger than a bottle, and made of leather or earthenware. Fr. *flacon.*

monster -- A thing to be wondered at; something of an unnatural size or shape; anything horrible. Lat. *monstrum,* from *monstrare,* to show; originally an omen; something unlucky; hence an unnatural or evil thing, a monster.

Polyphemus -- The Son of Neptune and the nymph Thoosa. He dwelt in a cave on Mount Etna.

Neptune -- Called Poseidon by the Greeks, was brother of Jupiter and Pluto, and ruled the sea in which he generally dwelt. He rode over it in a chariot, made of a shell, drawn either by winged horses, with brazen hoofs and golden manes, or by dolphins. It became smooth at his approach, whilst the whales and other monsters of the deep sported round him. He carried a trident or triple-pointed spear, made by the Cyclops, with which he shook the earth, called forth storms, or shattered rocks. He sided with the Greeks against Troy, but Ulysses incurred his anger for the injury inflicted on his son Polyphemus.

Agamemnon -- The grandson of Atreus, but according to Homer the son, king of Mycenæ, and the most powerful prince in Greece. He led the expedition, and brought 100 ships against Troy. He is the most majestic figure among the Greek chiefs, and one of the bravest in the field. After the fall of Troy he returned with the captive princess Cassandra, daughter of Priam; but they were killed by his wife Clytemnestra and his cousin Ægisthus.

Atreus -- Son of Pelops, grandson of Tantalus, and king of Mycenæ. The history of the house of Atreus was exceedingly tragic, and gave material for some of the finest works of the tragic Greek poets.

Jove -- Jupiter, the Greek Zeus. He was saved from destruction by his mother, as Saturn, his father, devoured all his male children. She took him to Mount Ida in Crete, where he was fed on the milk of a goat. When a year old he released his father who was imprisoned by the Titans. Saturn afterwards conspired against him, was driven from his kingdom, and Jupiter divided his dominions with his brothers, Pluto and Neptune. Jupiter was "sire of gods and men," the fountain of law and order, the avenger of wrongs, the dispenser of awards and punishments.

heartening -- (From heart.) Encouraging, animating, emboldening.

threshold -- The plank or stone underlying a door at the entrance of a house or other building; hence the entrance itself. O.-E. *threswold;* from A-S. *threscan,* to thresh, and *wold* wood, the word literally meaning a piece of wood for threshing on.

ambiguous -- See later note [ambiguously delivered]

made knots of osier twigs -- Knotted the osier twigs together. Osier is the water-willow whose twigs are used in making baskets. Fr. *osier.*

execrable rout. -- Hateful, or detestable rabble, or crowd.

"Which that abhorr'd man
No-Man did put out,
Assisted by his execrable rout."

CHAPMAN

bark. -- Any small vessel. Fr. *barque.*

ebb -- A reflux or flowing backward. The wave raised by the rock bore back the ship to the shore.

Laertes -- Father of Ulysses and king of Ithaca. He ceded the kingdom to his son, and was alive when Ulysses returned from Troy.

waster of cities --

"City racer," "city ruiner."

CHAPMAN.

Æolus -- According to Homer, he was ruler of the Æolian Islands (the Lipari), north-east of Sicily, to whom was given dominion over the winds. He invented sails, taught the art of navigation, and the nature of the winds, and in later times was regarded as a god and king of the winds which he kept enclosed in a mountain.

western wind -- Zephyrus, the west wind, was the son of Aurora, the goddess of the morning, and was said to produce flowers and fruits by the sweetness of his breath. Any mild gentle breeze is poetically called a zephyr.

"As gentle
As zephyrs blowing below the violet."

SHAKESPERE, Cymbeline, iv. 2.

tracked -- A nautical term meaning drawn by a line, or towed; hence sailed with difficulty.

passport -- Originally a permission to sail from, or into, a port or harbour. Fr. *passeport,* from *passer,* to pass, and *port.*

avaunt -- Begone, depart. Fr. *avant.*

"*Avaunt,* and quickly quit my land of thee,
Thou worst of all that breathe. It fits not me
To convoy, and take in, whom heavens expose.
Away, and with thee go the worst of woes.
That seek'st my friendship, and the gods thy foes."

CHAPMAN.

convoy -- To conduct, to escort, or bring on the way for protection. Fr. *convoyer,* from Lat, *on,* and *via* way.

will have perish, -- will, or determine, that they should perish.

Lamos -- Lamus, the capital of the country of the Læstrygones; so called after their king of that name, the son of Neptune.

Læstrygonians -- The Læstrygonians, the most ancient inhabitants of Sicily, were a savage race of cannibals of gigantic stature, who dwelt in the east or north coast. They destroyed eleven of Ulysses' ships, and he escaped with but one.

Antiphas -- Antiphates, King of the Læstrygones.

harpoon -- A spear or javelin thrown by hand, used to kill large fish. Fr. *harpon.*

"They were, like fishes, by the monsters slain
And borne to sad feast."

CHAPMAN.

Ææa -- A mythical island to the west of Italy, so-called from an island and a town in Colchis. (See Circe)

"Then to the isle *Ææa* we attain'd
Where fair-haired, dreadful, eloquent Circe reigned."

CHAPMAN.

Eurylochus -- The companion of Ulysses. He was prudent at the house of Circe, but not so when they came to the Triangular island, where he slew the sacred oxen of Apollo, and was in consequence shipwrecked.

Before her gate -- This sentence is loosely written: for "as" read "such as;" and for "of," read "from being," or "though."

ramped -- *Ramp* means to spring, or bound, or paw, standing on the hind legs. Fr. *ramper,* to creep.

"So on these men, the wolves and lions *ramp'd,*
Their horrid paws set up."

CHAPMAN.

loom -- A frame of wood in which cloth is woven. Old Eng. *lame.*

Smyrna -- A seaport of Nonia, and one of the most ancient and flourishing cities of Asia Minor. It is beautifully situated on a gulf of the same name, and the mountain slopes and fertile valley near it produced rich grapes from which its celebrated wine was made. It was, and continues to be, a great centre of trade between Europe and Asia. It stood highest in its claims as being the birth-place of Homer.

sorceries -- Enchantments; witchcrafts. Old Fr. *sorcerie,* from Lat. *sors, sortis,* a lot, fate, destiny.

mast -- The fruit of the beech or other forest tree.

"Oak-mast and beech, and kernel fruit they eat."

CHAPMAN.

apparition -- An unexpected appearance. Lat. *apparitio.*

Mercury -- The Greek Hermes, son of Jupiter. He was the herald or messenger of the gods, and was the god of eloquence, since heralds had to speak in important assemblies; hence the tongues of animals were offered to him in sacrifice. He invented the lyre, the reed pipe, the alphabet, and many other things. He was very cunning and skilful, and was the god of thieves. He is represented with wings on his hat and feet, carrying in his hand his caduceus, a rod entwined by two serpents, given to him by Apollo. He favoured the Greeks at Troy.

moly -- This was a fabulous plant, of mysterious power, having a black root and white blossom, given by Mercury, and by which Ulysses was able to counteract the magic spells of Circe as here described. Milton refers to this in *Comus*, 1. 636:

"Yet more med'cinal is it than that *moly*
That Hermes (Mercury) once to wise Ulysses gave."

clouted -- Patched, or mended with leather or other material. From A-S. *clut*, a little cloth, a patch. "And old shoes and clouted upon their feet." --Joshua, ix. 5.

blight -- The word is generally applied to those diseases in plants which cause the whole or part to wither and decay, whether arising from insects, fungi, or bad weather.

mildew -- A powdery growth, or minute fungi on plants, fruits, leather, or other things, diseased or decaying. A. -S. *meledeaw*, honeydew; probably from the sticky honey-like appearance of some kinds of blight.

charming-rod -- A rod used by wizards or magicians in exercising magical or supernatural powers. Moses and the magicians cast their rods before Pharaoh, and they became serpents.

Fates -- The Fates, or Parcæ, were three in number--Clotho, Lachesis, and Atropos. Clotho, the youngest, presided over birth, holding a distaff in hand; Lachesis held the spindle, and spun out the events and actions; and Atropos, the eldest, held a shears, and cut the threads of human life. They exercised vast power, and were subject to none of the gods except Jupiter, and, according to some, not even to him.

Styx -- The principal river in the nether world, which flowed round it seven times. It was called after Styx, the daughter of Oceanus, because she brought her children to Jupiter to assist him against the Titans. The most solemn oaths were sworn by her, and when one of the gods took such an oath, Iris fetched a cup of water from the Styx, and the god poured it out while taking the oath. If the oath was violated, Jupiter compelled the foresworn to drink of the Styx, and he was rendered senseless or oblivious for a year.

daughters to ... fountains, &c. -- The nymphs were a very numerous class of divinities, and may be divided into nymphs of the water and nymphs of the land. Of the former there were Oceanides and Nereides of the sea, and Naiades of rivers, lakes and springs. There were several classes of the latter--the Dryades presiding over woods. They were young and beautiful maidens, and were worshipped by the ancients, though not so solemnly as the greater deities. (See Calypso)

"Four handmaids served her there,
That daughters to her silver fountains were,
To her bright sea-observing sacred floods,
And to her uncut consecrated woods."

CHAPMAN.

aromatic -- A fragrant plant or drug, a perfume, or agreeable odour. Gr. *apomatikos*

regale -- A princely or magnificent feast. Fr. *regal*.

metamorphosis -- A Greek word meaning change of form or shape; from *meta*, beyond, over, and *morpho*, shape.

Hades -- Or Pluto, the god of the nether regions. He was son of Saturn and brother of Jupiter and Neptune, and obtained the kingdom of hell in the division of the world among the brothers. He was fierce and inexorable, and kept the gates of the lower world closed, that no spirits might return to earth. His abode being dark and gloomy, the goddesses refused to marry him, so he carried away Proserpine, daughter of Ceres, making a passage through the earth, and she became his queen. He wore a helmet made by the Cyclops which rendered him invisible, and he is described as sitting on a throne of sulphur, with his wife Proserpine, and the dog Cerberus at his feet. In later times the name Hades was transferred to his kingdom, the house of death.

Tiresias -- The most celebrated soothsayer in ancient times who abode in Thebes. He lived to a very great age, and was blind from his seventh year. Some say that Jupiter bestowed on him the gift of prophecy, and permitted him to live for seven or nine generations of men. Others consider that Minerva gave him the power of understanding the voices of birds, and a staff with which he could walk as safely as with his eyesight. During his life he was an infallible oracle to all Greece. He is said to have met his death by drinking the cold water of a fountain. In the lower world Homer gives him his prophetic power, and brings Ulysses to him for counsel.

poplar -- A tree of very rapid growth. Its wood is soft, and there are several kinds, as the black, the aspen, &c. Old Fr. *poplier*; Lat. *populus*, the poplar.

willows pale -- The willow is poetically associated with sorrow and woe. Chapman has "Tall firs and sallows (willows) that their fruits soon loose."

Prosperpine -- The daughter of Ceres, the goddess of earth. As she was gathering flowers, according to the Latin writers, in the fields of Sicily, Pluto appeared through the earth, and carried her to the infernal regions, where she became his wife and queen of hell. Her mother, disconsolate at her loss, searched the world for her for nine days. The Sun revealed to her where her daughter was, and she appealed to Jupiter for redress; but Prosperpine could not return, as she had eaten a pomegranate given by Pluto. She was allowed, however, to spend part of the year with her mother and the remainder with Pluto. She was universally worshipped by the ancients as the majestic queen of the souls of the dead. (See Hades)

Pyriphlegethon, Cocytus, Acheron -- Three rivers of hell. The two latter were rivers in Epirus, and were supposed to be connected with the lower regions, and hence they came to be described as being in the lower world. Homer makes Cocytus a tributary or branch of the Styx.

cubit -- A measure of about 18 inches, taken from the elbow to the tip of the middle finger. Lat. *cubitum* from *cubare* to lie down, the elbow being used for leaning upon.

Triangular island -- Trinacra, Trinacria, the ancient name of Sicily; "the three-forked island" (Chapman), so called from its shape. The earliest inhabitants were the Cyclops and Laestrygones. It was celebrated for its corn, and sacred to Ceres. Here Helios (in later times identified with Apollo), the God of the Sun, kept his sacred herds of oxen, attended by his daughter. He gave light to gods and men. Rising in the East from Oceanus, he traversed the heavens with chariot and horses, and descended into Oceanus in the West. He saw and heard all things, and his worship in Greece existed from very early times.

ambiguously delivered -- Having a doubtful or uncertain meaning. Lat. *ambiguus*, from *ambigere* to wander about with irresolute or uncertain mind. Lamb departs slightly here from his original. Tiresias' prophecy was not ambiguous. He warned Ulysses strongly against touching the oxen of the Sun; that by force or cunning he should with slaughter free his house of all the spoilers; after which he should make another voyage, and offer special sacrifice to Neptune to appease his anger.

Alcmena -- Daughter of Electryon, King of Mycenæ, and mother of Hercules by Jupiter.

Hercules -- The most celebrated of all the ancient heroes, and whose deeds were known throughout the old world. Jupiter announced on the day of his birth a hero would be born who would rule over the race of Perseus. Juno contrived that Eurystheus, grandson of Perseus, should be born first, to whom Hercules became subject. He served him for twelve years, and executed what are known as the twelve labours of Hercules, being fully supplied with arms by favour of the gods. He performed many other great deeds, and when he died was immortalized and worshipped as a god.

Leda... Tyndarus -- Leda was the wife of Tyndarus, King of Sparta, and mother of Castor and Clytemnestra by him, and Pollux and Helen by Jupiter. When Castor and Pollux were received among the immortals, Tyndarus surrendered the kingdom to Menelaus.

Helen -- The daughter of Jupiter and Leda, and the most beautiful woman of her time. When a child she was carried away by Theseus to Attica, but was recovered by her brothers, Castor and Pollux, and brought back to Sparta. She was sued by all the great Greek princes (see Introd.), and married Menelaus. During the Trojan War she sympathised with the Greeks, but married Deiphobus, the brother of Paris, on his death in the 9th year, and betrayed him to the Greeks on the fall of the city. She became reconciled to Menelaus, and returned with him to Sparta, and survived him. Various accounts are given of her death, after which she was honoured as a goddess.

Castor and Pollux -- (See Leda). Castor was skilled in the management of horses, and Pollux in boxing and wrestling. They were the patron deities of mariners, and Jupiter is said to have placed them among the stars as Gemini (the Twins). Castor was killed in a quarrel, and Pollux, being immortal, through grief at the loss of his brother, asked Jupiter either to take away his life or grant immortality to Castor. Jupiter gave him permission to share his fate and live alternatively with him, one day in the lower world and the other among the gods.

Iphimedeia -- wife of the giant Aloeus, and mother of Otus and Ephialtes by Neptune.

Otus and Ephialtes -- Usually called Aloidæ from their reputed father Aloeus. When nine years old they were 9 cubits in breadth and 37 in height, and threatened the gods with war. They would have accomplished this, according to Homer, if they had reached manhood:

"But Jove's son (Apollo) deprived
Their limbs of life, before the age that begins
The flower of youth, and should adorn their chins."

CHAPMAN

Ossa -- A mountain in Thessaly, connected with Pelion, and separated from Olympus by the Vale of Tempe, which was an act of Hercules, according to some traditions. It and Pelion were once the home of the Centaurs, a race half man and half horse.

Olympus -- The eastern part of the chain of mountains, running west and east, that formed the boundary of ancient Greece. It is 9,700 feet high, and covered with perpetual snow. It was the home of the gods, where they were shut in by a wall of clouds, the Horæ or Hours, goddesses of the seasons, keeping the gates. There was no rain, or wind, but an eternal spring existed.

Pelion -- Also a lofty mountain in Thessaly. The attempt made by the giants was to place Ossa on the slope of Olympus, and Pelion upon Ossa, so as to scale the top of Olympus and reach the abode of the gods. Pelion was covered with woods, and here the wood of the spear of Achilles was cut down, which none but himself could wield.

striplings -- *Strip*, and the diminutive ending *ling*, as being a small strip from the main stem. Hence a youth or growing boy. "Inquire thou whose son this *stripling* is." 1 Sam. xvii. 56.

Phædra -- Daughter of Minos, King of Crete, and wife of Theseus. She falsely accused her step-son, Hippolytus, and he was banished by his father. His horses were frightened by a sea-monster sent ashore by Neptune, and he was trampled beneath their feet, and crushed to death under his chariot wheels. Phædra, at his tragic fate, confessed her wickedness, and hung herself in despair.

Procris -- Daughter of Erechtheus, King of Athens, and wife of Cephalus. They loved each other with much affection, but Procris, fearing the love that Aurora had for her husband, watched him jealously when he went out hunting, and was accidentally killed by him with an unerring spear, given to her by the goddess Diana.

Ariadne and Theseus -- Ariadne was daughter of Minos, King of Crete. Theseus was a celebrated hero of ancient Greece, desirous of emulating Hercules. He was the son of Ægeus, King of Athens. Minos tyrannously exacted yearly seven chosen youths and seven maidens from the Athenians, to be sent to Crete to be devoured by the Minotaur, a terrible monster which he kept confined in a labyrinth. Theseus went as one of the youths, and assisted by Ariadne, who fell in love with him, he killed the Minotaur, and escaped by a clue of thread through the windings of the labyrinth. He carried Ariadne along with him, but according to Homer, she was killed on the island of Naxos by Diana. On approaching Athens he neglected to hoist the white sail which was to have been the signal of the success of his enterprise, and his father, thinking he had failed and was lost, cast himself into the sea, and hence the name Ægean Sea.

Eriphyle -- Wife of Amphiarus, a hero of Argos, who hid himself that he might not accompany an expedition, celebrated as the "Seven against Thebes," knowing that those engaged in it would be killed. Eriphyle, bribed by a golden necklace, discovered where her husband was. He commanded his son to murder his mother on hearing of his death. When this was known, the injunction was obeyed, and Eriphyle was murdered by her son.

"Loath'd Eriphyle,
That honour'd gold more than she loved her spouse."

CHAPMAN.

Egisthus -- Son of Thyestes, and nephew of Atreus. The latter brought him up as a son, but Ægisthus murdered Atreus because he ordered him to slay his father. He aided Clytemnestra in the murder of her husband, Agamemnon; but they were afterwards murdered themselves by her son Orestes.

training me forth -- Leading, or drawing along, in a solemn manner.

Clytemnestra -- Daughter of Tyndarus and Leda, and wife of Agamemnon. She was false to her husband while he was at Troy, and on his return, assisted by Ægisthus, she murdered him either at a feast prepared to celebrate his return, according to Homer, or as he was coming out from his bath. (See Ægisthus and Agamemnon.)

cast a foul aspersion -- Cast foul slander or censure, like sprinkling a body with foul water. From Lat. *aspergere*, to sprinkle, or scatter.

Icarius, Penelope -- Icarius was a Lacedemonian, and brother of Tyndraus, and father of Penelope. There were many suitors for her hand, and Ulysses is said to have won her in a foot-race. (See also Introd.) Icarius wished them to remain with him, and, on Ulysses' refusal, appealed to Penelope, who blushed and covered her face with her veil, intimating her desire to follow Ulysses. Icarius erected a statue to modesty on the spot where she then stood. Tormented by the suitors during the absence of Ulysses at Troy, she delayed them by promising to declare her decision when she had finished a robe she was weaving for her father-in-law, Laertes, and undid at night the work done during the day. Homer speaks highly of her:

"Exceedingly wise she is, and wise in good,
Icarius' daughter, chaste Penelope."

CHAPMAN

Telemachus -- Son of Ulysses and Penelope. He went in search of his father towards the close of his wanderings, visiting the courts of Nestor and Menelaus, accompanied by Minerva under the form of Mentor, and, returning to Ithaca, found him, and assisted in the slaughter of the suitors.

Orestes -- (See Ægisthus and Clytemnestra.) After the murder of his mother, Orestes was tormented by the Furies, but was purified by Apollo. After many adventures he became King of Mycenæ and Argos, and married Hermione, daughter of Menelaus, she having first, it is said, murdered her husband Neoptolemus, son of Achilles. He died at an advanced age by the bite of a serpent.

fame -- Rumour or public report. Lat. *fama*. "The fame thereof was heard in Pharoah's house" -Gen. xlv. 16.

Orchomen -- An ancient and wealthy city in Boeotia, on the river Cephissus, containing a celebrated temple to the Graces. It was very powerful at the time of the Trojan War.

Pylus -- There were three towns of this name which have been disputed as being the city of which Nestor was king. The Pylos on the Bay of Navarino, on the promontory west of the Gulf of Koron, seems to have the best claim.

Sparta -- Also called Lacedæmon, the chief city of Peloponnesus, was situated on the Eurotas, twenty miles from the sea. It was founded by Lacedæmon, son of Jupiter, who married Sparta, and named the city after her, who was daughter of Eurotas, after whom the river was called. Here Menelaus was king, and on the marriage of his daughter Hermione with Orestes, son of Agamemnon, the kingdoms of Sparta and Argos were united. The city stood on a plain, shut in on the east and west by mountains, and was six miles in circumference. Its inhabitants were renowned for their bravery, their discipline and valour in war, their love of liberty, and their aversion to idleness and luxury. They reared their children with great austerity, and a Spartan mother would slay her son if he brought shame on his country through cowardice, or honour with a festival his death as a hero.

Achilles -- Son of Peleus, King of the Myrmidons in Thessaly and the Nereid Thetis. His mother, in order to render him immortal, dipped him in the Styx, and succeeded in all parts of the body except the heel by which she held him. He led the Myrmidons, and brought 50 ships against Troy. He was the handsomest and bravest of all the Greeks. In the ninth year of the war he quarrelled with Agamemnon concerning a captive, and retired from the siege in anger. Homer's *Iliad* commences with this incident. He permitted his friend Patroclus to take his place in the combat and to wear his armour, and he being killed by Hector, Achilles rejoined the Greeks, having received new armour from Vulcan. He killed Hector, tied the body to his chariot, and dragged it round the walls of the city in sight of the

Trojans. He fell at the Scæan gate, pierced in the heel by an arrow shot by Paris, but directed by the hand of Apollo.

Thetis -- One of the fifty Nereides, daughters of Nereus, and wife of Peleus. Her wedding was honoured by the attendance of all the gods except Discord, who threw an apple amongst them, with the words "to the fairest" written on it, which gave rise to so much misery to the Greeks and Trojans. (See Introd. and Achilles)

Peleus -- King of the Myrmidons in Thessaly, and grandson of Jupiter, husband of Thetis, the only one among mortals who married an immortal. He was one of the Argonauts, but was too old to accompany to Troy his son Achilles, whose death he survived.

Neoptolemus -- Son of Achilles, brought up at the court of his grandfather, Lycomedes the King of Scyros, from whence Ulysses fetched him, and where he before had found Achilles in woman's attire among the daughters of the king. Neoptolemus fought with great bravery, and killed Priam at the taking of the city. He married Hermione, daughter of Menelaus, on his return to Greece, but was soon after killed by her or Orestes, and was buried at Delphi.

Scyros -- An island in the Ægean Sea, east of Negropont. Here Thetis concealed Achilles to save him from the fate that awaited him at the Siege of Troy.

conceit -- Quickness in understanding and seeing the meaning of things; active imagination. Lat. *conceptus.* "There's no more conceit in him than is in a mallet." 2 Hen. IV., ii. 4.

Ajax -- Son of Telamon, King of Salamis. He brought twelve ships against Troy, and was second only to Achilles in bravery and all the heroic qualities. On the death of Achilles he contended unsuccessfully with Ulysses for his armour, which Homer here gives as the cause of his death. Rushing from his tent in a fit of madness he slew the sheep of the Greek camp, think they were his enemies, and then took his own life. The blood that flowed to the ground was changed into the flower hyacinth.

despite -- Jealous spite, anger, or rage. Lat. *despectus,* contempt. "With all thy depite against the land of Israel." -- Ezekiel, xxv. 6.

Telamon -- King of Salamis, brother of Peleus, and father of Ajax. He was one of the Argonauts, and a friend of Hercules, and joined him in several expeditions.

Minos -- The son of Jupiter, and king and law-giver of Crete. For his justice, moderation, and wisdom, he was made judge of the lower regions. He was represented as sitting on a throne, with a sceptre in his hand. He heard the pleadings of the dead, shook the fatal urn, and dealt out their destinies.

Orion -- A great giant hero in Boeotia. He was a beautiful youth, was devoted to hunting, and lived in Crete with Diana. He was so tall that, standing in the middle of the sea, the waters only reached his shoulders. Various accounts are given of his death, some saying it was owing to his love for Aurora, or Diana's for him. When he died he was placed among the stars as a constellation, where he appears as a giant with a girdle, sword, a lion's skin, and a club.

Tityus -- Son of Terra (the earth), or of Zeus, according to some writers. He offended Latona, who called on her children for revenge, and they slew him with their arrows. He was then cast into the lower regions, and he was of such gigantic stature that he covered nine acres. His punishment was as here stated.

Latona -- The mother of Apollo and Diana, by Jupiter. Juno, through jealousy, drove her from heaven and persecuted her, allowing her nowhere to rest. At last she rested on the island of Delos (which see). Here Apollo and Diana were born; but she soon was obliged to fly from Delos, and wander over the world. Those who insulted her were severely punished either by Jupiter or her children. She afterwards became a powerful goddess.

Pytho -- The ancient name of Delphi. The Python was a serpent that lived in the caves of Mt. Parnassus, and which was sent after Latona by Juno to persecute her. It was slain by Apollo, and rotted at Delphi; hence its ancient name Pytho, and the Pythian games which commemorated this victory. It contained a great temple to Apollo and an oracle.

Panopeus -- An ancient town on the Cephissus in Phocis, north of the Gulf of Corinth.

fray -- Frighten, or alarm.

Tantalus -- Son of Jupiter, and father of Pelops and Niobe. He is variously stated as King of Lydia, Argos, or Corinth. Among the various accounts given of his crime is that referred to in the text. Wishing to try the divinity and power of the gods, he killed his son Pelops, and served the flesh in a banquet to them, as they stopped at his house on a journey. The word *tantalise* is derived from Tantalus.

"About his head, on high trees, clust'ring hung
Pears, apples, granates, olives, ever young
Delicious figs, and many fruit trees, more
Of other burden... The winds from sight
In gloomy vapours, made them vanish quite."

CHAPMAN

doom -- Judgment, or sentence. A-S. *dom*.

Sisyphus -- Son of Æolus, and founder of Corinth. He was the most crafty king of the heroic ages, and promoted commerce and navigation. For his wicked life he was terribly punished in the lower world. Various accounts are given of his special offence, the betrayal of the designs of the gods being one.

"There saw I Sisyphus in infinite moan,
With both hands heaving up a massy stone...
To wrest up to a mountain-top his freight;
When prest to rest it there, his nerves quite spent,
Down rushed the deadly quarry....
The sweat came gushing out from every pore,
And on his head a standing mist he wore,
Reeking from thence, as if a cloud of dust
Were raised about it."

CHAPMAN

Pirithous -- Son of Ixion or Jupiter, and King of the Lapithæ, a people in the mountains of Thessaly. He led them in a celebrated war against the Centaurs, a race half man and half horse, in which the latter were defeated. He became a great friend of Theseus. He attempted to carry away Proserpine from the nether world, in which Theseus assisted. They were caught by Pluto and kept in punishment, but Hercules delivered Theseus.

Scylla and Charybdis -- These were two rocks in the Straits between Italy and Sicily. In a cave in that nearest Italy dwelt Scylla, daughter of Cratæis, a terrible monster, who had twelve feet and six heads, each containing three rows of teeth, and who barked like a dog. Under a great fig-tree on the other and lower rock dwelt Charybdis, who thrice daily swallowed the waters, and thrice threw them up again. Circe is said to have poisoned the waters of the fountain where Scylla, once a beautiful maiden, bathed, thus converting her into a frightful monster. The ancient mariners feared the rock of Scylla, and the whirlpool of Charybdis; hence the proverb when one is in doubt between two difficulties or dangers, "between Scylla and Charybdis."

Sirens -- There were three Sirens, daughters of one of the Muses, who dwelt on the island of Caprea, on the west coast of Italy. The lower part of their bodies was that of a bird. Some suppose this form was given by Circe as a punishment for not preventing the carrying off of Proserpine by Pluto. They were told they were to perish if anyone escaped being charmed by their enchanting songs; and, disappointed at the escape of Ulysses, they cast themselves into the sea.

The call of any Siren --

"Whomsoever shall. . . but hear *the call*
Of any Siren, he will so dispose
Both wife and children, for their sorceries,
That never home turns his affections stream,
Nor they take joy in him, nor he in them."

CHAPMAN.

Invitement -- Invitation. The word is not now used.

Fen -- Low-lying land covered wholly or partially at times with water. A.-S. *fen*, marsh, or mud.

Argo -- The Argonauts, "the sailors of the Argo," a ship of fifty oars, so called because built by Argus, son of Phrixus, were the heroes of the first naval expedition, and went to recover the golden fleece. A king of Iolcus in Thessaly, named Pelias, usurped the crown from his brother, Æson, and in order to get rid of his son Jason, persuaded him to go to Colchis for the golden fleece, which was guarded by a dragon, and to avenge on King Æetes the death of their kinsman Phrixus. All the great heroes of the time, numbering fifty, went on the expedition. Jason performed many great labours, like those of Hercules. Assisted by Medea, the daughter of Æetes, who was greatly skilled in magic, he succeeded in obtaining the golden fleece, and after many trials returned to Iolcus with Medea, whom he married. This expedition occurred many years before the Trojan war.

The golden fleece -- Phrixus and Helle were the children of Athamas, King of Thebes. Their stepmother, Ino, afterwards the marine deity, intended to sacrifice them to Jupiter. They escaped, riding through the air on the back of a ram with a golden fleece and wings. On the way Helle fell into the sea and was drowned from whence the Hellespont was named. Arriving at Colchis, Phrixus sacrificed the ram, and Æetes hung the golden fleece on an oak in the grove of Mars, and according to some writers, murdered Phrixus.

Dolphin -- A fish of the whale tribe. There are several species, and they average from six to ten feet in length. They swim with great rapidity, bounding out of the sea, and showing great muscular power. They breathe through their lungs, and come to the surface at short intervals.

Dog-fish -- The popular name for several species of the smallest of the shark tribe. They are cruel and voracious, and worthless as food.

Cratis, or Cratæis -- Mother of Scylla by Phorcys, a sea deity.

Fore wind -- A favourable wind driving the ship by its impulse in its own direction. The adjective fore is largely used in sailor's language: e.g. fore bow, fore cabin, fore sheets, fore shore, &c.

"Come here, thou, worthy," &c. Chapman's Translation of the *Odyssey*, Book xii., lines 272-283.

heaven drowsy with the harmony -- Shakespeare, *Love's Labour's Lost*, iv. 3.

swart -- Swarth. A-S., *sweart*, of a dark colour.

frayed -- Frightened. These are old words; Lamb was much given to their use, being deeply versed in old English literature. (See fray.)

swoopt -- Swoop is akin to the verb sweep, and means to fall on and catch up while on the wing, as a hawk would a bird. Scylla's long necks would appear to have acted thus.

black night -- Nox, the personification of night, was one of the most ancient and the earliest of created deities. A black sheep was offered to her; also a cock, as the bird that in the darkness proclaims the coming day. She was represented as riding in a chariot covered with a veil bespangled with stars, the constellations as her messengers going before her.

severally -- Separately, or singly, one by one.

Apollo -- Son of Jupiter and Latona, and born at Delos. In the time of Homer he was distinct from Helios or the Sun, but in later times became identified with him. He had many great attributes. He shot the arrows of death; he averted evil; he was the god of prophecy, and spoke through the oracles; the god of song and music; the god of flocks and herds; the god of civil institutions. His worship had more influence on the Greeks than that of any other deity.

prospective penitence -- Future regret, pain or sorrow of heart.

nostril -- Old Eng. *nosethril*, nose and *thril* or *thyrl*, a hole. A-S., *nasthyrl*.

prodigy -- Something extraordinary, or out of the ordinary course of nature, from which an omen might be drawn. Lat. *prodigium*.

omen -- A sign by which a future event is foretold. Lat. *omen*. The signs might be good or bad; if the former, courage and hope were stimulated; if the latter, the evil threatened might be averted by sacrifices or some other means. The belief in omens has existed in all ages and countries, and lingers yet among the peasantry of civilized nations.

cable -- Usually a strong rope to hold a ship at anchor; here the ordinary ship's rope or rigging. Fr. *câble*; derived from Lat. *capere*, to take, or lay hold of.

bolt -- Thunder-bolt or streak of lightning.

sea-mew -- Sea-gull.

Ogygia -- A fabulous island, and according to Homer in the centre of the sea; but later writers place it east of the south promontory of Italy in the Ionian Sea.

alder -- Literally "the water-tree," a tree usually growing in moist land. A-S., *aler*.

balm-gentle -- A fragrant garden herb; the melissa officinalis, or balm-mint.

"A grove grew
In endless spring about her cavern round,
With odorous cypress, pines, and poplars, crown'd..
A vine did all the hollow cave embrace,
Still green, yet still ripe bunches gave it grace.
Four fountains, one against another, pour'd
Their silver streams; and meadows all enflower'd
With sweet *balm-gentle*, and blue violets hid,
That deck'd the soft breast of each fragrant mead."

CHAPMAN.

Mentor -- A faithful friend of Ulysses, to whom was entrusted the affairs of his home while he was absent at Troy. He had the charge of Telemachus, and when the latter set out on his journey in search of Ulysses, Minerva accompanied him in the form of Mentor acting the part of a wise and prudent guide and counsellor, and to such the name has since come to be applied. Telemachus' visit to Calypso is not from Homer. It is an invention of Fenelon's in *Les Aventures de Télémaque*.

stipulation -- Bargain, or agreement. Originally a money transaction: from *stips, stipis*, a gift in small coin.

Twelve months -- Ulysses remained seven years with Calypso in the island of Ogygia.

Jove ordered Mercury -- The ruler of gods and men shows evenhanded justice in the treatment of Ulysses. He assisted Neptune in punishing him for depriving the sea-god's son of his eye, and now he assists Minerva to rescue him from the snares of Calypso.

Pieria -- A mountainous district to the east of Olympus, in the south-east corner of Macedonia.

"He stoop'd *Pieria*, and thence
Glid through the air, and Neptune's confluence
Kiss'd as he flew, and check'd the waves as light
As any sea-mew in her fishing flight."

CHAPMAN.

mandate -- A command by authority; an official order. Lat. *mandatum*.

shipwright -- A *wright*, or maker, of ships.

In four days' time a ship was made -- It was not a ship, but a raft, according to Homer; one man could not do much at building a ship in four days.

Pleinds, or Pleiades -- A group of seven stars, of which six are visible to the naked eye. The word is from *plein*, to sail, as their rising indicates the time of safe navigation. They were the daughters of Atlas and Pleione, a daughter of Oceanus. They were said to have made away with themselves through grief at the loss of their sisters, the Hyades, or of their father, Atlas. They, as well as the Hyades, were placed among the stars.

Bear -- The Great Bear, also called Charles' Wain or Waggon, and The Plough, a constellation of seven stars near the North Pole of the heavens. In spring this constellation is in the zenith, and maybe said to be following Orion. In northern latitudes, beyond 40 degrees it "keeps above the ocean," for it never dips into the sea. Callisto, an Arcadian nymph, was beloved by Jupiter, who, to conceal this from Juno, changed her into a bear. Juno caused Diana to slay her in the chase, and Jupiter placed her among the stars, as the Great Bear.

Bootes -- That is "the ox-driver;" the imaginary figure of Bootes, supposed to be driving the team; hence "the Waggoner." In latitudes above 40 degrees north this constellation just sets, and does so very slowly. Arcas, son of Callisto, when hunting, was on the point of slaying her when he was prevented by Jupiter, who, some say, placed both among the stars.

"He beheld the Pleiades;
The Bear surnam'd the Wain, that round doth move
About Orion, and keeps still above
The billowy ocean; the slow setting star
Bootes call'd, by some the Waggoner."

CHAPMAN.

Phæacia -- The Phæaces were a fabulous people, in the island of Phæacia, also called Scheria, situated on the western parts of the world. They were a very luxurious people, and the term Phæax was applied to a glutton. The island is by some identified with Coroyra, the modern Corfu, one of the Ionian group.

Æthiopians -- People of Æthiopia, a term indefinitely applied to the country south of Egypt. The worship of Neptune was much observed by the people of Africa.

Solymi -- The people of Lycia, a district in the south of Asia Minor, and so called from the Solyma mountains. They were a brave and warlike race, and take a prominent place in Homer.

trident -- A sceptre or spear, with three prongs, the usual symbol of Neptune's power, made for him by the Cyclops. Lat. *tri*, and *dens*, a tooth.

cope -- The arch, or expanse of heaven, akin to cap, a covering.

"All earth took into the sea with clouds, grim Night
Fell tumbling headlong from the *cope* of light."

CHAPMAN

sail-yards -- The pieces of timber attached to the masts by which the sails are extended.

Boreas, Notus, Eurus, Zephyrus -- The north, south, east, and west winds, sprung from Astræus, a Titan, and Aurora, the goddess of the morning.

"Now Boreas
Toss'd it to Notus, Notus gave it pass
To Eurus, Eurus Zephyr made it pursue
The horrid tennis."

CHAPMAN

tennis -- A game with rackets and ball, in which the ball is being continually held in motion by striking it. Lat. *tenere*, to hold.

Ino Leucothea -- Daughter of Cadmus, and second wife of Athamas, King of Thebes. (See golden fleece.) Athamas, in a fit of madness, killed one of her sons, and she to escape her husband's fury threw herself and the other into the sea, and they became deities by the pity of Neptune.

Cadmus -- Son of Agenor, King of Phoenicia. He went in search of his sister Europa, who had been carried off by Jupiter. Not finding her, he consulted the oracle at Delphi, and was told to follow a certain cow and sacrifice it, and build a town on the spot. This he did, and reached Boeotia where the cow fell. He sent his men to a well, sacred to Mars, and they were eaten by a dragon. He slew the dragon, and on the advice of Minerva sowed its teeth, out of which sprung armed men. They killed each other, except five, who assisted him to build a city. This was Thebes, and they were the ancestors of its inhabitants. He married Harmonia, and gave her the necklace fatal to those who owned it.

cormorant -- Fr. *cormoran*, from Lat. *corvus marinus*, the sea-raven; a web-footed bird, and very gluttonous. It is trained in China to fish for its owner.

buffeted -- Beaten, slapped or cuffed. Old Fr. *buffet*, a slap in the face. "Then did they spit in His face, and *buffeted* Him." --Matthew xxvi. 67.

better parent -- His native country was more to him, and held in higher estimation than his parents.

distempers -- Social disorders.

mpending -- Overhanging. Lat. *impendere*, to hang.

main -- The ocean or open sea, as distinguished from a branch of it.

Minerva -- Called by the Greeks Athena, the goddess of wisdom. She sprang from the brain of Jupiter, and was worshipped in all parts of Greece. She was the preserver of the state; the patron of agriculture, inventions, arts, and industries; and the sustainer of law, order, and justice among men. She is usually represented as wearing a helmet, highly ornamented, holding a shield with the fearful head of Medusa on it, her garments being a sleeveless tunic and a cloak. She favoured the Greeks at Troy, and specially protected Ulysses.

Medusa -- One of the Gorgons. Her head was crowned with hissing serpents, and all who looked on it were turned into stone. (See similitude later.)

Calliroe -- The original means "at the mouth of a fair-flowing river," and Chapman probably took the epithet for the name of the river.

rack -- An instrument for stretching or extending anything; an engine of torture on which the body was stretched and tightly roped, and then drawn gradually until the limbs were dislocated.

ow trees -- Owing to their exposed condition, trees near a coast are generally low and short in growth.

billet -- A small log or piece of wood. Fr. *billot.*

Alcinous -- The son of Nausithous, the son of Neptune. Alcinous married Arete, his niece, the daughter of his brother, Rhexenor. They had five sons and one daughter, Nausicaa. He received Ulysses with great kindness, and heard the recital of his adventures, which occupies books vi., xiii. of the Odyssey. Lamb arranges the story in a consecutive form.

vestment -- A garment, dress, or robe; now usually applied to a priest's robes. Lat. *vestimentum*, from *vestire*, to clothe.

housewifery -- The business management of a house by the mistress.

council -- Here means consultation; the act of deliberating and advising on important matters. Lat. *concilium*, from con, and ciere , to move, or call.

"Satan... void of rest
His potentates to council called by night."

MILTON.

Senate -- A body of the most distinguished citizens, who assisted in consulting and deliberating on state affairs. Lat. *senatus*, from *senex*, old, or advanced in years.

"She chanced to find
Her father going abroad, to council call'd
By his grave senate."

CHAPMAN.

wardrobe -- A closet, or press, for keeping clothes. From word and robe: ward, from A-S. *weard*, guard or keeper.

nuptials -- Marriage, the marriage ceremony. Lat. *nuptiæ*, from *nubere*, to cover or veil, from the custom of covering the head of the bride with a veil.

Diana -- The Greek Artemis, the goddess of the chase or hunting. She was daughter of Jupiter and Latona, the twin sister of Apollo, and born in Delos. (See Latona). She represented, as a female divinity, the same idea as Apollo, a male divinity, represented. When he became identified with the sun, she became identified with the moon. As a huntress she was represented with bow, quiver, arrows or spear, and attended with dogs. As goddess of the morn, she was covered with a veil and large robe, and above her head a crescent. With Apollo, she sided with the Trojans

ebb -- The outline or exterior of a body or figure. Lat. *lineamentum*, from *linea*, a line.

stature -- Originally an upright posture; the natural height of the human body. Lat. *statura*.

features -- The fashion, make, or general cast of a face; hence the face or countenance, generally speaking. Old Fr. *faiture*, from Lat. *facere*, to make.

Delos -- The smallest of the Cyclades, a group of islands in the Ægean Sea. It was said to have been raised by the trident of Neptune, and floated until fixed to the bottom of the sea by Jupiter with adamantine chains as a resting-place for Latona when pursued by the jealous envy of Juno. Here Apollo and Diana were born, and it became specially sacred to Apollo. It had a great temple raised for his worship, which contained an oracle. It was visited by pilgrims from all quarters; and the island was held so sacred, that all human and animal remains were removed from it, and no births or deaths were allowed to occur there.

cruel habit of calamity -- Owing to his long and repeated sufferings, he easily gave way to his overstrained feelings.

"But for me, A cruel habit of calamity Prepared the strong impression thou hast made."

CHAPMAN.

monster -- (See monster above.)

admired -- Wondered. Lat. *admirari*, to wonder.

entered the city -- Homer tells that Ulysses, as he entered the city, was met by Minerva in guise of a city maiden, carrying a pitcher. She "about him a darkness cast" to avoid observation, gave him particulars of the king and queen, and advised him how to proceed.

rampires -- Rampart; that which fortifies or defends a place from assault; a mound of earth or fortifying wall. Fr. *rempart*. The word rampire is now obsolete.

"*Rampires* so high, and of such strength withal,
It would with wonder any eye appal."

CHAPMAN.

Demodocus -- A celebrated minstrel at the court of King Alcinous.

oracle -- A special spot chosen by a deity as an abode, from which answers might he given to an inquiring worshipper. The answers were generally vague, or of doubtful meaning, and might agree with varied results or events. The inquiry was usually made respecting an enterprise, war, or impending battle. Lat. *oraculum*, from *oro*, to speak; *os oris*, the mouth.

Pytho -- (See Pytho above.).

period -- The end or termination of their wars in Troy. Gr. *periodos*, a going round, a space of time; from *peri*, round, and *odos*, a way; hence, the completion or end of a space of time, or set of events.

strategem -- A plan or scheme in war for deceiving an enemy.

weed -- An article of clothing; generally an outer garment or cloak. A-S. *weed*.

libation -- Before drinking it was usual to pour some of the wine on the ground as an offering to the gods. Lat. *libare*, to pour out as an offering.

games of strength -- Athletic training and contests were universally practised in ancient Greece. The games and trials of strength were very varied, but did not include combats with weapons. Four great national athletic festivals were held periodically--the Olympic, Pythian, Isthmian, and Nemean games. The first was the most ancient, and the only prize given to the conqueror was a garland of wild olive, which was reckoned as the highest reward in life, the winner being held in great estimation as having brought honour to his country or city.

quoit -- A circular piece of metal or stone, usually ring-shaped, used to pitch at a mark. It was the discus of the ancients.

javelin -- A short spear or lance generally thrown by the hand. Fr. *javeline*.

pageant -- A spectacle or show got up for the entertainment of a distinguished person. The etymology is doubtful.

Deiphobus -- Son of Priam, King of Troy, and the bravest of the Trojans after Hector. He married Helen after the death of Paris. On the fall of the city his house was among the first that was sacked and burned. Helen is said to have betrayed him to Menelaus, who slew him, and fearfully mangled his body.

conceit -- Thought, idea, or image. Lat. *conceptus*.

pusillanimous -- Unmanly; wanting in firmness or strength of mind. Lat. *pusillanimis*; from pusus, diminutive of puer, a boy, and animus, the mind.

policies -- Clever or cunning schemes, stratagems or wiles. Lat. *politia*, the condition of a state; from Gr. *polis*, a city.

fame -- (See fame above.).

passport -- (See passport above.).

admiration -- Wonder. (See admired above).

quick-sand -- A mass of sand mixed with water, having little or no consistency, and unable to sustain much weight. Quicksands occur at the mouths of rivers, or on coasts, and are very dangerous.

strife of joys -- Lamb follows Chapman here so closely that the passage is a little obscure. It would be clearer if expressed negatively. "So may all the gods not bless me with the strife of joys (conflicting joys) if I do not acknowledge," &c.

'Nausicaa! Flower of all this empery! (kingdom)
So Juno's husband, that the strife for noise
Makes in the clouds, bless me with *strife of joys*,
In the desired day that my house shall show,
As I, as I to a goddess there shall vow,
To thy fair hand that did my being give,
Which I'll acknowledge every hour I live."

CHAPMAN.

flecker -- To streak or stripe, to spot.

massy -- Massive. The word is now seldom used.

curveting -- Leaping, bounding, the up-and-down motion of the vessel, like the particular action of a horse called *curvet*.

nymphs, Naiads -- A nymph was a goddess of the waters, mountains, or woods. Lat. *nympha*. Gr. *nymphe* (See daughters... above).

turrets -- Little towers; small erections attached to a building, and rising above it. Lat. *turris*, a tower.

turned to stone -- Neptune was specially angry with the Phæces, who were descended from him, for helping Ulysses. He said:--

"No more the gods shall honour me,
Since men despise me, and those men that see
The light in lineage of mine own loved race...
But now this curious built Phæacian ship,
Returning from her convoy, I will strip
Of all her fleeting matter, and to stone
Transform and fix it."

CHAPMAN

rocky and barren -- Compare:--

"Rocky 'tis and rough. . . the compass is not great,
The little yet well-filled with wine and wheat,
It feeds a goat and ox well, being still
Water'd with floods, that ever over-fill
With heaven's continual showers; and wooded so,
It makes a spring of all the kinds that grow.
...'Tis Ithaca."

CHAPMAN

Crete -- The ancient name of Candia. It was early inhabited by a civilised people, and is said to have had one hundred cities. It was famous for the laws made by King Minos.

vouchsafed -- Condescended, graciously granted or permitted. From vouch and safe, to vouch or answer for safety.

saving him unseen -- That is, saving him, she remaining unseen.

counterfeit views -- Apparent, not real; having the appearance or show of wisdom only, but not wisdom itself.

Nerytus -- A mountain in the north of the island of Ithaca.

"Here Mount Neritus shakes his curled tress of shady woods."

CHAPMAN

suitor -- One who woos or solicits a woman in marriage.

profaning -- Treating with disrespect; undue familiarity; debasing. Lat. *pro*, before, and *fanum*, temple; that is, without the temple, unholy.

son's adventures -- (See Mentor above).

divine impression -- The change of form that Minerva was about to make.

scrip -- A small bag, wallet, or satchel. Used several times in the Bible. 1 Sam. xvii. 40, Matthew x, 10, &c.

And in requital ope his leathern *scrip*."

MILTON, Comus, 1. 626.

mendicant -- One who begs alms. Lat. *mendicare*, to beg.

Eumæus -- The faithful swineherd of Ulysses. His father was king of the island of Syrie in the Ægean sea, and he was taken away by Phoenician sailors, and sold as a slave to Laertes, the father of Ulysses.

that majesty -- Ulysses.

"Here I lie
Grieving and mourning for the *majesty*
That, god-like, wonted to be ruling here."

CHAPMAN.

requite -- Repay; reward. Formed from the prefix *re*, and *quit*, to satisfy or pay an obligation, claim, or debt.

our fare.., lean beasts -- That is, the flesh of the lean beasts is the fare of poor herdsmen. The sense is clearer in Chapman:--

"Eat now, my guest, such lean swine as are meat
for us poor swains."

surfeits -- Excesses in eating and drinking. Old Fr. *surfait*, from *sur*, over, and *faire*, to do.

raiment -- Clothing; shortened from arraiment, from array.

stick to invent -- Not hesitate, or stop, to invent.

"These travellers, for clothes, or for a meal,
At all adventures, any lie will tell.
Nor do they trade for truth. Not any man...
Did ever tell her any news, but lies."

CHAPMAN.

vulture -- A large rapacious bird of prey found in the East. Its beak is large and strong, the head and neck without feathers, but having a collar of long feathers at the root. It detects its prey a long way off. Lat. *vultior*.

Idomeneus -- Son of Deucalion, and grandson of Minos, King of Crete. He was a suitor to Helen, and led the Cretans with eighty ships against Troy. He was one of the bravest of the heroes, and, according to Homer, returned safely to his country after the fall of the city.

Thesprotia -- A country on the coast of Epirus, west of Greece, nearly opposite the island of Corfu. It was called after the Thesprotians, its most ancient inhabitants.

Dodona -- This oracle was in Thesprotia. It was dedicated to Jupiter, and was one of the most famous in Greece. The answers were given from lofty trees, the rustling of the wind through the branches, and the contact of the brazen vessels hung on them, being interpreted by the priests.

carcase -- A dead body. From Old Eng. *carcays*, from Old Fr. *carquasse*, a framework, case, or shell; hence the body itself.

"If your king return not, let your servants throw
My old limbs headlong from some rock most high,
That other poor men may take fear to lie."

mantle -- A loose garment or cloak worn over other garments. Lat. *mantellum.*

Strong liquor...prefer a speech -- Compare:--

"Strong wine commands the fool and moves the wise,
Moves and impels him too to sing and dance,
And break in pleasant laughters, and perchance,
Prefer (deliver or address) a speech too that were better in."

ambush -- To lie in wait in order to surprise an enemy. The proper meaning is a hiding in a wood. It is a corruption of an older word embush, to be in a wood.

bitter freezing night -- In eastern countries the nights are often very cold and frosty. This is due to the rapid radiation of heat from the earth and atmosphere into a cloudless sky. The presence of clouds prevents the heat from radiating into space, and thus renders the temperature higher than in their absence.

bulrush -- (From *bull*, in the sense of large and rush.) A kind of large rush growing in wet land or water. Chapman has *osiers* and reeds.

moat -- Here used in a military sense, meaning the deep trench or ditch around the walls of a city or castle, and usually filled with water. The word originally meant a hill, mound, or bank of earth, and is still so applied as an antiquarian term, which in time became transferred to the ditch.

jogged -- Pushed with the elbow or hand; called attention to.

"I *jogg'd* Ulysses, who lay passing near,
And spake to him, that had a nimble ear."

nimble -- Lively, quick in motion.

servitor -- One who serves. In Oxford University the term is applied to a student partly supported by the college funds, whose duty formerly was to wait at table. Fr. *serviteur,* from Lat. *servire,* to serve.

"Their delights are far from being given
To such grave *servitors.* Youths richly trick'd
In coats or cassocks, locks divinely slick'd,
And looks most rapting, ever have the gift
To taste their crown'd cups, and full trenchers shift."

trencher -- A large wooden plate for table use on which food was formerly cut. Fr. *tranchoir,* from *trancher,* to cut or carve.

brags himself -- Boasts himself.

"From ample Crete he boasts himself."

wolfish inclination -- Savage inclination. It is an unusual expression; but Lamb here closely follows Chapman.

"Methinks, a *wolfish power*

My heart puts on to tear and to devour,
To hear your affirmation."

Arcesius -- Son of Jupiter, father of Laertes, and grandfather of Ulysses.

'Only to the king,
Jove-bred Arcesius did Laertes spring;
Only to old Laertes did descend
Ulysses; only to Ulysses' end
Am I the adjunct, whom he left so young,
That from me to him never comfort sprung."

CHAPMAN.

dogs. . . saw the goddess -- It is popularly understood to this day, that the presence of ghosts or supernatural beings is felt by dogs and other animals.

decrepit -- Broken down with age; literally noiseless, or creeping about quietly like old people. From Lat. *decrepitus*; from de, not, and crepare, to rattle, to make a noise.

refrain -- Keep back.

admire -- (See admired above.)

substantially -- Actually or really existing in substance, the literal meaning of the word.

'In him his father shone *substantially* expressed."

MILTON, *Paradise Lost*, Bk. iii., 1. 140.

law of her free power -- It is enacted that she may exercise such power freely.

"'Tis within the *law*
Of her free power. Sometimes to show me poor,
Sometimes again thus amply to restore
My youth and ornaments, she still would please.
The gods can arise, and throw men down with ease."

CHAPMAN.

nuptials -- (See nuptials above.)

Dulichium -- The largest of a group of islands at the mouth of the Achelous opposite Ithaca. It was supposed they were originally nymphs, and were thus transformed for neglecting sacrifices to the god of the river. Dulichium at the present day is united to the mainland.

Samos -- An island off the west coast of Asia Minor, separated from it by a narrow strait. It was celebrated in later times for its art, science, and splendid buildings; and its chief city Samos was considered one of the finest in the world. The island is about eight miles in circumference, and very fertile.

Zacynthus -- The modern Zante, an island off the west coast of Greece, one of the Ionian group. It was celebrated in ancient times for its pitch wells, and it still yields bitumen. Homer calls it the "woody Zacynthus."

king of skies -- Jupiter.

'Thinkest thou, if Pallas (Minerva) and the *King of Skies*
We had to friend, would their sufficiencies
Make strong our part? Or that some other yet
My thoughts must work for."

sufficiency -- Power, capacity, or ability to help.

contumelious -- Insolent; rudely contemptuous, or abusive.

expostulate -- To reason earnestly with.

alms -- Anything given in charity. A-S. *almes*; Old Eng. *almesse*. The word was formerly used in the singular number, as Acts iii. 3: "asked an alms;" but it is now generally used in the plural.

humours -- State of mind, temper, or mood. Fr. Lat. *humere*, to be moist. It originally meant moisture, particularly that of animal bodies, and was applied as a medical term to secretions in the body; hence it once expressed mental depression or melancholy, arising from a disordered condition of the body. (See spleen below.)

Antinous -- A native of Ithaca, the most determined tormentor of Ulysses and the first of the suitors that was killed by him.

vagabond -- One wandering from place to place without a settled home, and usually applied to such a person not having an honest way of living. Lat. *vagabundus*, from *vagari*, to stroll or wander about.

travelling Egyptian -- This does not mean a gypsy. They were first known about the fourteenth century. Ulysses, in a speech immediately before, said he had come from Egypt and Cyprus, to which Antinous replied:--

"Stand off, nor profane
My board so boldly, lest I show thee here
Cyprus and Egypt made more sour than there.
You are a saucy set-faced *vagabond*."

board -- A table used for setting food on.

"Beggars at your board, I perceive, should get
Scarce salt from your hands, if themselves brought meat."

husband -- A man wedded to a wife. It originally meant the head or master of a house; from A-S. *hûs*, house, and *bonda,* a peasant or owner of a farm. Hence, it easily passed to its present meaning.

Irus -- The coward beggar of Ithaca. His real name was Arnæus, but, as the common messenger of the suitors, he was called Irus.

egged -- Urged or edged on. From A-S. *ecgan*, to sharpen.

Olympic and Pythian games -- Two of the four great national festivals of Greece (see games above), but which did not exist in Homer's time. The Olympic was the most ancient and celebrated, and was held every four years at Olympia, on the banks of the river Alpheus in Elis, and near the Temple of Jupiter. The Pythian games were said to be founded in commemoration of the victory of Apollo over the Pytho, a great serpent that lived in the caves of Mount Parnassus. They were held every third year in a plain near Delphi.

brawny -- Strong, fleshy, muscular. Brawn, the flesh of the hoar, also meant the muscular part of the body, but is not now commonly so used. "His breast so broad and *brawny*."-- Chapman. Old Fr. *braon*, the fleshy part of the body.

sinew -- That which unites a muscle to a bone. Used here to express muscular development. A-S., *sinewe*.

Echetus -- A cruel king of Epirus, on the north-west coast of Greece.

spectacle -- Something to gaze at.

coward -- A person without courage. Old Fr. *couard*. The word is usually explained as having been originally applied to an animal that drops his tail, as a dog; the word *couard* was also applied as an old hunting term to a hare.

taken the foil -- Taken the defeat.

Eurymachus -- One of the chief suitors to Penelope.

sleek -- Smooth; hence glossy. Old Eng. *slik*.

glory -- The light surrounding the head of a person of great sanctity; usually figured in pictures by rays of gold, &c.

"Some god doth bear
This man's resemblance, for, thus standing near
The glistering torches, his slick'd head doth throw
Beams round about as these cressets (lamps) do."

CHAPMAN.

task-work -- Work done and paid for by the piece.

glebe land -- Fertile, fruitful. The word is now usually restricted to land yielding an income to a parish church. Lat. *gleba*, a clod or soil.

bout -- A contest. It is another form of *bought*, an obsolete word meaning bend or twist. *Bout* means a turn or round of work, as in mowing or reaping; hence, a contest, a trial, as wrestling, fencing, drinking bouts.

massy -- (See massay above.)

profaned -- (See profaning above).

spleen -- Malice, spite, or envy. The spleen, which is an organ in the stomach, was long considered to be the seat of ill-humour, bad emotions, and melancholy. To express these qualities, the terms "spleen" and "humours" were usually applied to men, and the similar term "vapours" to women. (See humours below.)

armoury -- A place where arms or weapons of war are kept for safety.

omen -- (See omen above.)

housewiveries -- (See housewifery above.)

stress of weather -- Violent winds or tempests.

guest-rites -- The ceremonies or duties observed in entertaining a guest or visitor.

"Whom my home received with *guest-rites*."

CHAPMAN.

painting -- This word is often applied to a description in words, whether spoken or written.

"Thus many tales Ulysses told the wife,
At most but *painting*, yet most like the life."

kindly -- According to the kind or nature; natural, the original meaning. "The *kindly* fruits of the earth." -- *Book of Common Prayer.*

bridle -- A check or restraint. This and the word *curb,* the strap and chain which restrain and govern the horse, are used in the sense of governing and restraining the passions or emotions of the mind.

dreamed a dream -- In all ages and countries the idea has prevailed that future events might be foretold by means of dreams. Interpreters of dreams were held in high estimation in early times of, of which Joseph in Egypt is an example. Here Penelope discerning the wisdom of Ulysses, considered his great foresight might be able to forecast the events implied in the dream.

soused -- Here means swooped or fell suddenly, as a bird on its prey. The word is used intransitively here. The transitive verb means to plunge into water or drench; also, to steep in pickle.

trussing -- Applied to the action of a hawk or other bird seizing its prey, and soaring with it into the air. The word in this sense is now obsolete.

"When straight a crook-beak'd eagle from a hill
Stoop'd, and *truss'd* all their necks, and all did kill."

CHAPMAN

death of sleep -- Compare:

"But none can live without the *death of sleep.*
Th" Immortals in our mortal memories keep
Our ends and deaths by sleep, dividing so
Our times spent here, to let us nightly try
That while we live, as much live as we die."

CHAPMAN

mess -- Food set down for one meal.

gall -- A bitter secretion from the liver in animals; hence anything very bitter, bitterness, rancour. (See spleen,).

Philætius -- A steward of Ulysses, who with Eumæus assisted him in destroying the suitors.

your meat drops blood -- These were signs of impending evil. (See omen.) The passage in Chapman runs as follows:--

"A night, with which death sees,
Your heads and faces hides beneath your knees;
Shrieks burn about you; your eyes thrust out tears;
These fixed walls, and the main beam that bears
The whole house up, in bloody torrents fall;
The entry full of ghosts stands; full the hail
Of passengers to hell; and under all
The dismal shades; the sun sinks from the poles;
And troubled air pours bane about your souls."

apparition -- A spirit, ghost, or phantom. (See apparition above.)

Theoclymenus -- A soothsayer who returned to Ithaca from Sparta with Telemachus.

imminent -- Threatening, full of danger, impending. Lat. *imminere,* to project or jut out.

banquet planet -- It was a common belief among the ancients, and continued down to recent times, that the stars exercised great influence over all human affairs. The character and career of men were largely determined by the particular star under which they were born. The star that ruled at the banquet would be said to have an evil aspect, and threaten destruction to the wooers.

Minerva. . .put into the mind of Telemachus -- Minerva put it into the mind of Penelope, and not into that of her son.

"Pallas, the goddess with the sparkling eyes,
Excites Penelope t" object the prize,
The bow and bright steels, to the wooer's strength.
.. And thus she spake:
: here propose divine Ulysses' bow
For that great master-piece to which ye vow.
He that can draw it with least show to strive,
And through these twelve axe-heads an arrow drive,
Him will I follow, and this house forego."

CHAPMAN.

comely -- Graceful; handsome. From *come*, in the sense of *become*, to be suitable. A-S. *cymlic*, suitable, fit. We say an article of dress becomes a person, or is becoming.

Colchos -- [Colchis] A country of Asia, bounded on the west by the Euxine or Black Sea, and on the north by the Caucasus. It was famous as the land to which the Argonauts voyaged. (See Circe above.) This speech was delivered by Eurymachus shortly after the contest of Ulysses with Irus.

unctuous -- Greasy, oily. From Lat. *unguere, unctum*, to anoint.

Liodes. . . Polybus, &c. Suitors to Penelope.

mastery -- Pre-eminence; superiority.

cunning -- Knowing; skilful; experienced. A-S. *cunnan*, to know. The word is now more generally used in a bad sense, as artful, sly, deceitful.

craft -- Trade; manual work. Like "cunning," it has fallen into a bad sense, as guile, deceit.

"Past doubt he is a man profess'd
n bowyers' (archers') craft, and sees quite through the wood;
Or something, certain, to be understood
There is in this his turning of it still.
A *cunning* rogue he is at any ill."

CHAPMAN.

plight -- Condition. "Sound *plight.*" --Chapman. Through the rest of this paragraph Lamb follows his author closely.

Phoebus -- Means Bright or Pure. The term was applied by Homer to Apollo, to signify the glory and the beauty of youth, and it remained when Apollo afterwards became identified with the Sun.

deadly arrow . . . lifting a cup. -- The death of Antinous gave rise to the proverb:

"There's many a slip
  Twixt the cup and lip."

The passage in Chapman is:--

"He said, and off his bitter arrow thrust
Right at Antinous, that struck him just
As he was lifting up the bowl, to show
That 'twixt the cup and lip much ill may grow."

destiny -- That which is fixed or determined; fate; doom. Lat. *destinare* to fix or determine. The Parcæ or Fates, who presided over human life, were called the Destinies. (See Fates above.)

horrid -- Qualified to strike terror, or excite horror. In the fight with the suitors Eumæus and Philætius also joined; and Minerva, as here described, gave great assistance.

frayed -- (See fray above.)

similitude -- Likeness or shape. Lamb is not quite accurate here, as she appeared thus to the suitors.

"Pallas took in hand
Her *snake-fring'd* shield, and on that beam took stand
In her true form, where swallow-like she sat.
And then, in this way of the house and that,
The wooers, wounded at the heart with fear,
Fled the encounter."

CHAPMAN.

snake-fringed shield -- The shield of Minerva was represented with the dying head of Medusa, the Gorgon, with the hissing serpents twining round it. Anyone who looked upon the Gorgon was turned into stone. Perseus was given a mirror by Minerva in which he could look with safety, and finding Medusa asleep he slew her, and Minerva fastened her head upon her shield. (See Minerva above.)

prediction of Tiresias -- (See Tiresias and Mentor above.)

asseveration -- Positive statement or assertion.

Menelaus -- Son of Atreus, and husband of Helen. During the siege of Troy he distinguished himself by his bravery in battle. He was one of those hidden in the wooden horse. He was among the first to leave Troy after its destruction, accompanied by Helen. He took eight years to reach his home, where he lived afterwards in great prosperity. (See Introduction and Leda above.)

world given them in fee -- Usually termed in *fee simple;* which means possession to a person and his heirs for ever.

THE END

Printed in Great Britain
by Amazon

18004376R00061